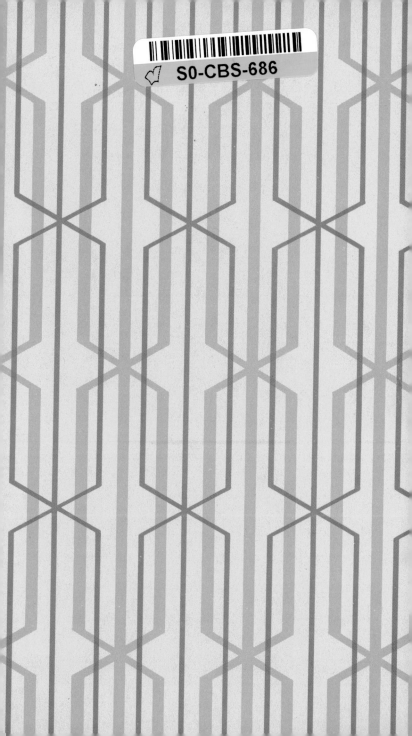

STORIES BY FOREIGN AUTHORS

♣

SPANISH

PÉDRO ANTONIO DE ALARCÓN

STORIES BY
FOREIGN AUTHORS

SPANISH

Short Story Index Reprint Series

BOOKS FOR LIBRARIES PRESS
FREEPORT, NEW YORK

First Published 1898

Reprinted 1970

STANDARD BOOK NUMBER:
8369-3368-0

LIBRARY OF CONGRESS CATALOG CARD NUMBER:
72-110211

PRINTED IN THE UNITED STATES OF AMERICA

CONTENTS

THE TALL WOMAN

BY

PÉDRO ANTONIO DE ALARCÓN

From " Modern Ghosts."   Translated by Rollo Ogden.

THE TALL WOMAN

BY PÉDRO ANTONIO DE ALARCÓN

I.

" HOW little we really know, my friends;
how little we really know."

The speaker was Gabriel, a distinguished civil
engineer of the mountain corps. He was seated
under a pine tree, near a spring, on the crest of
the Guadarrama. It was only about a league
and a half distant from the palace of the Escurial,
on the boundary line of the provinces of Madrid and Segovia. I know the place, spring, pine
tree and all, but I have forgotten its name.

" Let us sit down," went on Gabriel, " as that
is the correct thing to do, and as our programme
calls for a rest here—here in this pleasant and
classic spot, famous for the digestive properties
of that spring, and for the many lambs here de-
voured by our noted teachers, Don Miguel Bosch,
Don Máximo Laguna, Don Augustin Pascual, and
other illustrious naturalists. Sit down, and I will
tell you a strange and wonderful story in proof of
my thesis, which is, though you call me an ob-
scurantist for it, that supernatural events still occur on this terraqueous globe. I mean events

which you cannot get into terms of reason, or science, or philosophy—as those 'words, words, words,' in Hamlet's phrase, are understood (or are not understood) to-day."

Gabriel was addressing his animated remarks to five persons of different ages. None of them was young, though only one was well along in years. Three of them were, like Gabriel, engineers, the fourth was a painter, and the fifth was a *littérateur* in a small way. In company with the speaker, who was the youngest, we had all ridden up on hired mules from the Real Sitio de San Lorenzo to spend the day botanizing among the beautiful pine groves of Pequerinos, chasing butterflies with gauze nets, catching rare beetles under the bark of the decayed pines, and eating a cold lunch out of a hamper which we had paid for on shares.

This took place in 1875. It was the height of the summer. I do not remember whether it was Saint James's day or Saint Louis's; I am inclined to think it was Saint Louis's. Whichever it was, we enjoyed a delicious coolness at that height, and the heart and brain, as well as the stomach, were there in much better working order than usual.

When the six friends were seated, Gabriel continued as follows:

"I do not think you will accuse me of being a visionary. Luckily or unluckily, I am, if you will allow me to say so, a man of the modern world. I have no superstition about me, and am as much of a Positivist as the best of them, although I include among the positive data of nature all the mysterious faculties and feelings of the soul. Well, then, apropos of supernatural, or extra-natural, phenomena, listen to what I have seen and heard, although I was not the real hero of the very strange story I am going to relate, and then tell me what explanation of an earthly, physical, or natural sort, however you may name it, can be given of so wonderful an occurrence.

" The case was as follows. But wait ! Pour me out a drop, for the skin-bottle must have got cooled off by this time in that bubbling, crystalline spring, located by Providence on this piny crest for the express purpose of cooling a botanist's wine."

II.

" WELL, gentlemen, I do not know whether you ever heard of an engineer of the roads corps named Telesforo X——; he died in 1860."

"No ; I have n't."

" But I have."

" So have I. He was a young fellow from Andalusia, with a black moustache; he was to have married the Marquis of Moreda's daughter, but he died of jaundice."

"The very one," said Gabriel. "Well, then, my friend Telesforo, six months before his death, was still a most promising young man, as they say nowadays. He was good-looking, well-built, energetic, and had the glory of being the first one in his class to be promoted. He had already gained distinction in the practice of his profession through some fine pieces of work. Several different companies were competing for his services, and many marriageable women were also competing for him. But Telesforo, as you said, was faithful to poor Joaquina Moreda.

"As you know, it turned out that she died suddenly at the baths of Santa Águeda, at the end of the summer of 1859. I was in Pau when I received the sad news of her death, which affected me very much on account of my close friendship with Telesforo. With her I had spoken only once, in the house of her aunt, the wife of General Lopez, and I certainly thought her bluish pallor a symptom of bad health. But, however that may be, she had a distinguished manner and a great deal of grace, and was, besides, the only daughter of a title, and a title that carried some comfortable thousands with it; so I felt sure my good mathematician would be inconsolable. Consequently, as soon as I was back in Madrid, fifteen or twenty days after his loss, I went to see

him very early one morning.   He lived in elegant
bachelor quarters in Lobo Street—I do not remember the number, but it was near the Carrera
de San Jerónimo.

"The young engineer was very melancholy,
although calm and apparently master of his grief.
He was already at work, even at that hour, labor-
ing with his assistants over some railroad plans
or other.   He was dressed in deep mourning.

"He greeted me with a long and close embrace, without so much as sighing.   Then he
gave some directions to his assistants about the
work in hand, and afterwards led me to his pri-
vate office at the farther end of the house.   As
we were on our way there he said, in a sorrowful tone and without glancing at me :

"'I am very glad you have come.   Several
times I have found myself wishing you were here.
A very strange thing has happened to me.   Only
a friend such as you are can hear of it without
thinking me either a fool or crazy.   I want to get
an opinion about it as calm and cool as science
itself.

"'Sit down,' he went on when we had reached
his office, 'and do not imagine that I am going
to afflict you with a description of the sorrow I
am suffering—a sorrow which will last as long as
I live.   Why should I ?   You can easily picture
it to yourself, little as you know of trouble.   And
as for being comforted, I do not wish to be,

2

either now, or later, or ever !   What I am going to speak to you about, with the requisite deliberation, going back to the very beginning of the thing, is a horrible and mysterious occurrence, which was an infernal omen of my calamity, and which has distressed me in a frightful manner.'

"' Go on,' I replied, sitting down.   The fact was, I almost repented having entered the house as I saw the expression of abject fear on my friend's face.

"' Listen, then,' said he, wiping the perspiration from his forehead."

III.

"' I DO not know whether it is due to some inborn fatality of imagination, or to having heard some story or other of the kind with which children are so rashly allowed to be frightened, but the fact is, that since my earliest years nothing has caused me so much horror and alarm as a woman alone, in the street, at a late hour of the night.   The effect is the same whether I actually encounter her, or simply have an image of her in my mind.

"' You can testify that I was never a coward. I fought a duel once, when I had to, like any other man.   Just after I had left the School of Engineers, my workmen in Despeñaperros revolted, and I fought them with stick and pistol until

I made them submit. All my life long, in Jaen, in Madrid, and elsewhere, I have walked the streets at all hours, alone and unarmed, and if I have chanced to run upon suspicious-looking persons, thieves, or mere sneaking beggars, they have had to get out of my way or take to their heels. But if the person turned out to be a solitary woman, standing still or walking, and I was also alone, with no one in sight in any direction —then (laugh if you want to, but believe me) I would be all covered over with goose-flesh ; vague fears would assail me ; I would think about beings of the other world, about imaginary existences, and about all the superstitious stories which would make me laugh under other circumstances. I would quicken my pace, or else turn back, and would not get over my fright in the least until safe in my own house.

"'Once there I would fall a-laughing, and would be ashamed of my crazy fears. The only comfort I had was that nobody knew anything about it. Then I would dispassionately remind myself that I did not believe in goblins, witches, or ghosts, and that I had no reason whatever to be afraid of that wretched woman driven from her home at such an hour by poverty, or some crime, or accident, to whom I might better have offered help, if she needed it, or given alms. Nevertheless, the pitiable scene would be gone over again as often as a similar thing occurred—

and remember that I was twenty-four years old,
that I had experienced a great many adventures
by night, and yet that I had never had the
slightest difficulty of any sort with such solitary
women in the streets after midnight! But nothing of what I have so far told you ever came to
have any importance, since that irrational fear
always left me as soon as I reached home, or
saw any one else in the street, and I would
scarcely recall it a few minutes afterwards, any
more than one would recall a stupid mistake
which had no result of any consequence.

" ' Things were going on so, when, nearly three
years ago (unhappily, I have good reason for
knowing the date, it was the night of November
15–16, 1857), I was coming home at three in the
morning. As you remember, I was living then
in that little house in Jardines Street, near
Montera Street. I had just come, at that late
hour, a bitter, cold wind blowing at the time, out
of a sort of a gambling-house—I tell you this,
although I know it will surprise you. You know
that I am not a gambler. I went into the place,
deceived by an alleged friend. But the fact was,
that as people began to drop in about midnight,
coming from receptions or the theatre, the play
began to be very heavy, and one saw the gleam
of gold in plenty. Then came bank-bills and
notes of hand. Little by little I was carried
away by the feverish and seductive passion, and

lost all the money I had. I even went away owing a round sum, for which I had left my note behind me. In short, I ruined myself completely ; and but for the legacy that came to me afterwards, together with the good jobs I have had, my situation would have been extremely critical and painful.

" ' So I was going home, I say, at so late an hour that night, numb with the cold, hungry, ashamed, and disgusted as you can imagine, thinking about my sick old father more than about myself. I should have to write to him for money, and this would astonish as much as it would grieve him, since he thought me in very easy circumstances. Just before reaching my street, where it crosses Peligros Street, as I was walking in front of a newly-built house, I perceived something in its doorway. It was a tall, large woman, standing stiff and motionless, as if made of wood. She seemed to be about sixty years old. Her bold and malignant eyes, unshaded by eyelashes, were fixed on mine like two daggers. Her toothless mouth made a horrible grimace at me, meant to be a smile.

" ' The very terror or delirium of fear which instantly overcame me gave me somehow a most acute perception, so that I could distinguish at a glance, in the two seconds it took me to pass by that repugnant vision, the slightest details of her face and dress. Let me see if I can put together

my impressions in the way and form in which I
received them, as they were engraved ineffaceably
on my brain in the light of the street-lamp which
shone luridly over that ghastly scene. But I am
exciting myself too much, though there is reason
enough for it, as you will see further on. Don't
be concerned, however, for the state of my mind.
I am not yet crazy !

"'The first thing which struck me in that
woman, as I will call her, was her extreme height
and the breadth of her bony shoulders. Then,
the roundness and fixity of her dry, owl-eyes, the
enormous size of her protruding nose, and the
great dark cavern of her mouth. Finally, her
dress, like that of a young woman of Avapiés—
the new little cotton handkerchief which she
wore on her head, tied under her chin, and a
diminutive fan which she carried open in her
hand, and with which, in affected modesty, she
was covering the middle of her waist.

"'Nothing could be at the same time more
ridiculous and more awful, more laughable and
more taunting, than that little fan in those huge
hands. It seemed like a make-believe sceptre
in the hands of such an old, hideous, and bony
giantess ! A like effect was produced by the
showy percale handkerchief adorning her face
by the side of that cut-water nose, hooked and
masculine; for a moment I was led to believe (or
I was very glad to) that it was a man in disguise.

" ' But her cynical glance and harsh smile were those of a hag, of a witch, an enchantress, a Fate, a—I know not what! There was something about her to justify fully the aversion and fright which I had been caused all my life long by women walking alone in the streets at night. One would have said that I had had a presentiment of that encounter from my cradle. One would have said that I was frightened by it instinctively, as every living being fears and divines, and scents and recognizes, its natural enemy before ever being injured by it, before ever having seen it, and solely on hearing its tread.

" ' I did not dash away in a run when I saw my life's sphinx. I restrained my impulse to do so, less out of shame and manly pride than out of fear lest my very fright should reveal to her who I was, or should give her wings to follow me, to overtake me—I do not know what. Panic like that dreams of dangers which have neither form nor name.

" ' My house was at the opposite end of the long and narrow street, in which I was alone, entirely alone with that mysterious phantom whom I thought able to annihilate me with a word. How should I ever get home? Oh, how anxiously I looked towards that distant Montera Street, broad and well lighted, where there are policemen to be found at all hours! I decided, finally, to get the better of my weakness ; to dissemble and hide that wretched fear; not to hasten my pace, but to keep on advancing slowly, even at the cost of years of health or life, and in this way, little by little, to go on getting nearer to my house, exerting myself to the utmost not to fall fainting on the ground before I reached it.

"'I was walking along in this way—I must have taken about twenty steps after leaving behind me the doorway where the woman with the fan was hidden, when suddenly a horrible idea came to me—horrible, yet very natural nevertheless—the idea that I would look back to see if my enemy was following me. One thing or the other I thought, with the rapidity of a flash of lightning: either my alarm has some foundation or it is madness; if it has any foundation, this woman will have started after me, will be overtaking me, and there is no hope for me on earth. But if it is madness, a mere supposition, a panic fright like any other, I will convince myself of it in the present instance, and for every case that may occur hereafter, by seeing that that poor old woman has stayed in that doorway to protect herself from the cold, or to wait till the door is opened; and thereupon I can go on to my house in perfect tranquillity, and I shall have cured myself of a fancy that causes me great mortification.

"'This reasoning gone through with, I made

an extraordinary effort and turned my head.   Ah,
Gabriel!—Gabriel! how fearful it was! The
tall woman had followed me with silent tread,
was right over me, almost touching me with her
fan, almost leaning her head on my shoulder.

" ' Why was she doing it?—why, my Gabriel?
Was she a thief? Was the really a man in
disguise? Was she some malicious old hag
who had seen that I was afraid of her? Was
she a spectre conjured up by my very cowardice?
Was she a mocking phantasm of human self-de-
ception?

" ' I could never tell you all I thought in a
single moment.   If the truth must be told, I gave
a scream and flew away like a child of four years
who thinks he sees the Black Man.   I did not
stop running until I got out into Montera Street.
Once there, my fear left me like magic.   This in
spite of the fact that that street also was deserted.   Then I turned my head to look back to
Jardines Street.   I could see down its whole
length.   It was lighted well enough for me to see
the tall woman, if she had drawn back in any
direction, and, by Heaven! I could not see her,
standing still, walking, or in any way! However, I was very careful not to go back into that
street again.   The wretch, I said to myself, has
slunk into some other doorway.   But she can't
move without my seeing her.

" ' Just then I saw a policeman coming up

Caballero de Gracia Street, and I shouted to him
without stirring from my place. I told him that
there was a man dressed as a woman in Jardines
Street. I directed him to go round by the way
of Peligros and Aduana Streets, while I would
remain where I was, and in that way the fellow,
who was probably a thief or murderer, could not
escape us. The policeman did as I said. He
went through Aduana Street, and as soon as I saw
his lantern coming along Jardines Street I also
went up it resolutely.

"'We soon met at about the middle of the
block, without either of us having encountered a
soul, although we had examined door after door.

"'"He has got into some house," said the
policeman.

"'"That must be so," I replied, opening my
door with the fixed purpose of moving to some
other street the next day

"'A few moments later I was in my room; I
always carried my latchkey, so as not to have
to disturb my good José. Nevertheless, he was
waiting for me that night. My misfortunes of
the 15th and 16th of November were not yet
ended.

"'"What has happened?" I asked him, in
surprise.

"'"Major Falcón was here," he replied, with
evident agitation, "waiting for you from eleven
till half-past two, and he told me that, if you came

home to sleep, you had better not undress, as he would be back at daybreak."

"'Those words left me trembling with grief and alarm, as if they had predicted my own death to me. I knew that my beloved father, at his home in Jean, had been suffering frequent and dangerous attacks of his chronic disease. I had written to my brothers that, if there should be a sudden and fatal termination of the sickness, they were to telegraph Major Falcón, who would inform me in some suitable way. I had not the slightest doubt, therefore, that my father had died.

"'I sat down in an arm-chair to wait for the morning and my friend, and, with them, the news of my great misfortune. God only knows what I suffered in those two cruel hours of waiting. All the while, three distinct ideas were inseparably joined in my mind; though they seemed unlike, they took pains, as it were, to keep in a dreadful group. They were: my losses at play, my meeting with the tall woman, and the death of my revered father.

"'Precisely at six Major Falcón came into my room, and looked at me in silence. I threw myself into his arms, weeping bitterly, and he exclaimed, caressing me:

"'"Yes, my dear fellow, weep, weep."'"

IV.

"My friend Telesforo," Gabriel went on, after having drained another glass of wine, "also rested a moment when he reached this point, and then he proceeded as follows:

"'If my story ended here, perhaps you would not find anything extraordinary or supernatural in it. You would say to me the same thing that men of good judgment said to me at that time: that every one who has a lively imagination is subject to some impulse of fear or other; that mine came from belated, solitary women, and that the old creature of Jardines Street was only some homeless waif who was going to beg of me when I screamed and ran.

"'For my part, I tried to believe that it was so. I even came to believe it at the end of several months. Still, I would have given years of my life to be sure that I was not again to encounter the tall woman. But, to-day, I would give every drop of my blood to be able to meet her again.'

"'What for?'

"'To kill her on the spot.'

"'I do not understand you.'

"'You will understand me when I tell you that I did meet her again, three weeks ago, a few hours before I had the fatal news of my poor Joaquina's death.'

" 'Tell me about it, tell me about it !'

" 'There is little more to tell. It was five o'clock in the morning. It was not yet fully light, though the dawn was visible from the streets looking towards the east. The street-lamps had just been put out, and the policemen had withdrawn. As I was going through Prado Street, so as to get to the other end of Lobo Street, the dreadful woman crossed in front of me. She did not look at me, and I thought she had not seen me.

" 'She wore the same dress and carried the same fan as three years before. My trepidation and alarm were greater than ever. I ran rapidly across Prado Street as soon as she had passed, although I did not take my eyes off her, so as to make sure that she did not look back, and, when I had reached the other end of Lobo Street, I panted as if I had just swum an impetuous stream. Then I pressed on with fresh speed towards home, filled now with gladness rather than fear, for I thought that the hateful witch had been conquered and shorn of her power, from the very fact that I had been so near her and yet that she had not seen me.

" 'But soon, and when I had almost reached this house, a rush of fear swept over me, in the thought that the crafty old hag had seen and recognized me, that she had made a pretence of not knowing me so as to let me get into Lobo

Street, where it was still rather dark, and where she might set upon me in safety, that she would follow me, that she was already over me.

" ' Upon this, I looked around—and there she was ! There at my shoulder, almost touching me with her clothes, gazing at me with her horrible little eyes, displaying the gloomy cavern of her mouth, fanning herself in a mocking manner, as if to make fun of my childish alarm.

" ' I passed from dread to the most furious anger, to savage and desperate rage. I dashed at the heavy old creature. I flung her against the wall. I put my hand to her throat. I felt of her face, her breast, the straggling locks of her gray hair until I was thoroughly convinced that she was a human being—a woman.

" ' Meanwhile she had uttered a howl which was hoarse and piercing at the same time. It seemed false and feigned to me, like the hypocritical expression of a fear which she did not really feel. Immediately afterwards she exclaimed, making believe cry, though she was not crying, but looking at me with her hyena eyes :

" ' " Why have you picked a quarrel with me ? "

" ' This remark increased my fright and weakened my wrath.

" ' " Then you remember," I cried, "that you have seen me somewhere else."

" ' " I should say so, my dear," she replied, mockingly. " Saint Eugene's night, in Jardines Street, three years ago."

" ' My very marrow was chilled.

" ' " But who are you ? " I asked, without letting go of her. " Why do you follow me ? What business have you with me ? "

" ' " I am a poor weak woman," she answered, with a devilish leer. " You hate me, and you are afraid of me without any reason. If not, tell me, good sir, why you were so frightened the first time you saw me."

" ' " Because I have loathed you ever since I was born. Because you are the evil spirit of my life."

" ' " It seems, then, that you have known me for a long time. Well, look, my son, so have I known you."

" ' " You have known me? How long ? "

" ' " Since before you were born ! And when I saw you pass by me, three years ago, I said to myself, *that 's the one.*"

" ' " But what am I to you ? What are you to me ? "

" ' " The devil ! " replied the hag, spitting full in my face, freeing herself from my grasp, and running away with amazing swiftness. She held her skirts higher than her knees, and her feet did not make the slightest noise as they touched the ground,

"'It was madness to try to catch her. Besides, people were already passing through the Carrera de San Jerónimo, and in Prado Street, too. It was broad daylight. The tall woman kept on running, or flying, as far as Huertas Street, which was now lighted up by the sun. There she stopped to look back at me. She waved her closed fan at me once or twice, threateningly, and then disappeared around a corner.

"'Wait a little longer, Gabriel. Do not yet pronounce judgment in this case, where my life and soul are concerned. Listen to me two minutes longer.

"'When I entered my house I met Colonel Falcón, who had just come to tell me that my Joaquina, my betrothed, all my hope and happiness and joy on earth, had died the day before in Santa Águeda. The unfortunate father had telegraphed Falcón to tell me—me, who should have divined it an hour before, when I met the evil spirit of my life! Don't you understand, now, that I must kill that born enemy of my happiness, that vile old hag, who is the living mockery of my destiny?

"'But why do I say kill? Is she a woman? Is she a human being? Why have I had a presentiment of her ever since I was born? Why did she recognize me when she first saw me? Why do I never see her except when some great cal-

amity has befallen me? Is she Satan? Is she
Death? Is she Life? Is she Antichrist? Who
is she? What is she?'"

V.

"I WILL spare you, my dear friends," continued
Gabriel, "the arguments and remarks which I
used to see if I could not calm Telesforo, for they
are the same, precisely the same, which you are
preparing now to advance to prove that there is
nothing supernatural or superhuman in my story.
You will even go further; you will say that my
friend was half crazy; that he always was so;
that, at least, he suffered from that moral disease
which some call 'panic terror,' and others 'emo-
tional insanity'; that, even granting the truth of
what I have related about the tall woman, it must
all be referred to chance coincidences of dates
and events; and, finally, that the poor old creature could also have been crazy, or a thief, or a
beggar, or a procuress—as the hero of my story
said to himself in a lucid interval."

"A very proper supposition," exclaimed Gabriel's comrades; "that is just what we were
going to say."

"Well, listen a few minutes longer, and you
will see that I was mistaken at the time, as you
are mistaken now. The one who unfortunately
3

made no mistake was Telesforo. It is much easier to speak the word ' insanity ' than to find an explanation for some things that happen on the earth."

" Speak, speak ! "

" I am going to ; and this time, as it is the last, I will pick up the thread of my story without first drinking a glass of wine."

VI.

" A few days after that conversation with Telesforo I was sent to the province of Albacete in my capacity as engineer of the mountain corps. Not many weeks had passed before I learned, from a contractor for public works, that my unhappy friend had been attacked by a dreadful form of jaundice ; it had turned him entirely green, and he reclined in an arm-chair without working or wishing to see anybody, weeping night and day in the most inconsolable and bitter grief. The doctors had given up hope of his getting well.

" This made me understand why he had not answered my letters. I had to resort to Colonel Falcón as a source of news of him, and all the while the reports kept getting more unfavorable and gloomy.

" After an absence of five months I returned to

Madrid the same day that the telegraph brought the news of the battle of Tetuan. I remember it as if it were yesterday. That night I bought the indispensable *Correspondencia de España*, and the first thing I read in it was the notice of Telesforo's death. His friends were invited to the funeral the following morning.

"You will be sure that I was present. As we arrived at the San Luis cemetery, whither I rode in one of the carriages nearest the hearse, my attention was called to a peasant woman. She was old and very tall. She was laughing sacrilegiously as she saw them taking out the coffin. Then she placed herself in front of the pall-bearers in a triumphant attitude and pointed out to them with a very small fan the passage-way they were to take to reach the open and waiting grave.

"At the first glance I perceived, with amazement and alarm, that she was Telesforo's implacable enemy. She was just as he had described her to me—with her enormous nose, her devilish eyes, her awful mouth, her percale handkerchief, and that diminutive fan which seemed in her hands the sceptre of indecency and mockery.

"She immediately observed that I was looking at her, and fixed her gaze upon me in a peculiar manner, as if recognizing me, as if letting me know that she recognized me, as if acquainted with the fact that the dead man had told me about the scenes in Jardines Street and Lobo Street, as if defying me, as if declaring me the inheritor of the hate which she had cherished for my unfortunate friend.

" I confess that at the time my fright was greater than my wonder at those new *coincidences* and *accidents*. It seemed evident to me that some supernatural relation, antecedent to earthly life, had existed between the mysterious old woman and Telesforo. But for the time being my sole concern was about my own life, my own soul, my own happiness—all of which would be exposed to the greatest peril if I should really inherit such a curse.

" The tall woman began to laugh. She pointed at me contemptuously with the fan, as if she had read my thoughts and were publicly exposing my cowardice. I had to lean on a friend's arm to keep myself from falling. Then she made a pitying or disdainful gesture, turned on her heels, and went into the cemetery. Her head was turned towards me. She fanned herself and nodded to me at the same time. She sidled along among the graves with an indescribable, infernal coquetry, until at last she disappeared for ever in that labyrinth of tombs.

" I say for ever, since fifteen years have passed and I have never seen her again. If she was a human being she must have died before this ; if she was not, I rest in the conviction that she despised me too much to meddle with me.

"Now, then, bring on your theories! Give me your opinion about these strange events. Do you still regard them as entirely natural?"

THE WHITE BUTTERFLY

BY

JOSÉ SELGAS

Translated by Mary J. Serrano.

THE WHITE BUTTERFLY

BY JOSÉ SELGAS

BERTA has just completed her seventeenth year. Blissful age in which Love first whispers his tender secrets to a maiden's heart! But cruel Love, who for every secret he reveals draws forth a sigh! But here is Berta, and beside her is a mirror, toward which she turns her eyes; she looks at herself in it for a moment and sighs, and then she smiles. And good reason she has to smile, for the mirror reveals to her the loveliest face imaginable; whatever disquiet Love may have awakened in her heart, the image which she sees in the mirror is enchanting enough to dispel it.

And why should it not? Let us see. "What has her heart told her?" "It has told her that it is sad." "Sad! and why?" "Oh, for a very simple reason! Because it thrills in response to a new, strange feeling, never known before. It fancies—curious caprice!—that it has changed owners." "And why is that?" "The fact is, that it has learned, it knows not where, that men are ungrateful and inconstant, and this is the

reason why Berta sighs." "Ah ! And what does
the mirror tell her to console her ? " " Why, the
mirror tells her that she is beautiful." " Yes ? "
" Yes ; that her eyes are dark and lustrous, her
eyebrows magnificent, her cheeks fresh and
rosy." " And what then ? " " It is plain ; her
heart is filled with hope, and therefore it is that
Berta smiles."

This is the condition of mind in which we find
her.   Up to the present she has passed her life
without thinking of anything more serious than
the innocent pranks of childhood ; she was a
child up to the age of seventeen, but a boisterous, gay, restless, daring, mischievous child ; she
turned the house upside down, and in the same
way she would have been capable of turning the
world upside down ; she had neither fears nor
duties ; she played like a crazy thing and slept
like a fool.   For her mother had died before
Berta was old enough to know her ; and although
her mother's portrait hung at the head of her
bed, this image, at once sweet and serious, was
not sufficient to restrain the thoughtless impetu-
osity of the girl.   She was, besides, an only
daughter, and her father, of whom we shall give
some account later, adored her.   In addition to
all this, her nurse, who acted as housekeeper in
the house, was at the same time the accomplice
and the apologist of her pranks, for the truth is
she loved her like the apple of her eye.

Less than this might have sufficed to turn an angel into an imp, and indeed much less would have sufficed in Berta's case, for the natural vivacity of her disposition inclined her to all kinds of pranks. Opposition irritated her to such a degree as to set her crying. But what tears ! Suddenly, in the midst of her sobs, she would burst out laughing, for her soul was all gayety, spontaneous, contagious gayety, the gayety of the birds when day is breaking.

But this gayety could not last for ever; and, willing or unwilling, the moment had to come some time when Berta would quiet down ; for it was not natural that she should remain all her life a madcap; and this moment at last arrived ; and all at once the girl's boisterous gayety began to calm down, to cloud over, like a storm that is gathering, like a sky that is darkening.

The nurse is the first to observe this change in Berta, and although the girl's pranks had driven her to her wits' end, seeing her silent, thoughtful, pensive, that is to say, quiet, she is overjoyed. The girl is now a woman. Profound mystery ! She has left off the giddiness of childhood to take on the sedateness of youth. Poor woman ! she does not know that a young girl is a thousand times more crazy than a child. But the fact is that Berta does not seem the same girl. And the change has taken place of a sudden, from one day to another, in the twinkling of an eye, so to say.

And sedateness becomes her well, very well. She seems taller, more—more everything; nothing better could be asked of her; but since she has become sensible the house is silent. The songs, the tumult, all the boisterousness of the past have disappeared. The good nurse, who is enchanted to see her so quiet, so silent, so sedate, yet misses the noisy gayety that formerly filled the house; and if the choice had been given to her, she would hardly have known which to prefer.

In this way the days pass calm and tranquil. Berta, who had always been so early a riser, does not now rise very early. Does she sleep more? That is what no one knows, but if she sleeps more she certainly eats less; and not only this, but from time to time, and without any apparent cause, heart-breaking sighs escape her.

The nurse, who idolizes her, and who would do anything in the world to please or to serve her, observes it all but says nothing. She says nothing, but she thinks the more. That is to say, that at every sigh she hears she draws down her mouth, screws up her eye, and says to herself: " Hm ! there it is again."

Of course she would not remain silent for long; for she was not a woman to hold her tongue easily. Besides, Berta's sedateness was now getting to be a fixed fact, and the nurse was at the

end of her patience ; for as she was accustomed
to say, " A loaf that is put into the oven twisted
will not come out of it straight."

And if she succeeded in keeping silence for a
few days, it was only because she was waiting
for Berta herself to speak and tell her what was
on her mind ; but Berta gave no sign that she
understood her ; her heart remained closed to
the nurse, notwithstanding all her efforts to open
it. The key had been lost, and none of those
that hung at the housekeeper's girdle fitted it.
It would be necessary to force the lock.

One day the nurse left off temporizing and took
the bull by the horns. She entered Berta's room,
where she found her engaged in fastening a flam-
ing red carnation in her dark hair.

" There ! that 's what I like to see," she said.
" That 's right, now. What a beautiful pink ! It
is as red as fire. And pinks of that color don't
grow in your flower-beds ! "

Berta cast down her eyes.

" You think I can't see what is going on before
my eyes," she continued, " when you know that
nothing can escape me. Yes, yes. I should like
to see the girl that could hoodwink me ! But
why don't you say something ? Have you lost
your tongue ? "

Berta turned as red as a poppy.

" Bah ! " cried the nurse. " That pink must
have flown over from the terrace in front of your

windows. I can see the plant from here ; there were four pinks on it yesterday, and to-day there are only three. The neighbor, eh ? What folly ! There is neither sense nor reason in that."

This time Berta turned pale, and looked fixedly at her nurse, as if she had not taken in the sense of her words.

" I don't mean," resumed the nurse, " that you ought to take the veil, or that the neighbor is a man to be looked down upon either ; but you are worthy of a king, and there is no sort of sense in this. A few signals from window to window ; a few sidelong glances, and then—what ? Nothing. You will forget each other. It will be out of sight out of mind with both of you."

Berta shook her head.

" You say it will not be so ? " asked the nurse.

" I say it will not," answered Berta.

" And why not ? Let us hear why not ? What security have you—"

Berta did not allow her to finish.

" Our vows," she said.

" Vows ! " cried the nurse, crossing herself. " Is that where we are !—Vows ! " she repeated, scornfully ; " pretty things they are—words that the wind carries away."

Some memory of her own youth must have come to her mind at this moment, for she sighed and then went on :

" And would they by chance be the first vows

in the world to be broken ? To-day it is all very
well ; there is no one else for you to see but the
neighbor ; but to-morrow ? "

" Never," replied Berta.

" Worse and worse," returned the nurse ; " for
in that case he will be the first to tire of you, and
then hold him if you can. To-day he may be
as sweet as honey to you, but to-morrow it will
be another story. What are you going to say ?
That he is young, and handsome ? Silly, silly
girl. Is he any the less a man for that ? Do you
want to know what men are ? "

Berta, going up to her nurse, put her hand over
her mouth and answered quickly :

" No, I don't want to know."

The nurse left Berta's room, holding her hands
to her head and saying to herself :

" Mad, stark, staring mad ! "

We know already that Berta has a father, and
now we are going to learn that this father, without being in any way an extraordinary being, is
yet no common man. To look at him, one would
take him to be over sixty ; but appearances are
in this case deceitful, for he is not yet forty-nine.
In the same city in which he dwells live some
who were companions of his childhood, and they
are still young ; but Berta's father became a
widower shortly after his marriage, and the loss
of his wife put an end to his youth. He settled

his affairs, gave up his business, realized a part of his property and retired from the world. That is to say, that he devoted himself to the care of his daughter, in whom he beheld the living image of the wife he had lost. Why should he wish to be young any longer? He grew aged then long before he had grown old.

Berta—Berta. In this name all his thoughts were centred, and in his thoughts there was much of sweetness and much of bitterness, for there is not in the circle of human happiness a cup of honey that has not its drop of gall.

To see him now walking up and down his room, looking now at the ceiling, now at the floor, biting his nails and striking his forehead, one would think the heavens were about to fall down and crush him or the earth to open up under his feet.

Suddenly he struck his forehead with his open palm, and crossing over to the door of the room, he raised the curtain, put out his head, and opened his lips to say something; but the words remained unuttered, and he stood with his mouth wide open, gazing with amazement at the nurse who, without observing the movement of the curtain, was approaching the door, gesticulating violently; it was evident that she had something extraordinary on her mind.

Berta's father drew aside; the nurse entered the room, and the two remained face to face, looking at each other as if they had never seen each other before."

" What is the matter, Nurse Juana?" asked Berta's father. "I never saw you look like that before."

"Well, you look no better youself. Any one would say, to see you, that you had just risen from the grave."

Berta's father slowly arched his eyebrows, heaved a profound sigh, and sinking into a chair, as if weighed down by the burden of existence, he asked again :

" What is the matter ? "

"The matter is," answered the nurse, " that the devil has got into this house."

" It is possible," he answered ; " and if you add that it is not an hour since he left this room, you will not be far wrong."

" The Lord have mercy on us ! " exclaimed the nurse : " the devil here ! "

" Yes, Nurse Juana, the devil in person."

" And you saw him ? "

" I saw him."

"What a horrible visitor ! " exclaimed Juana, crossing herself.

" Nó," said Berta's father, " he is not horrible; he took the appearance of a handsome young man who has all the air of a terrible rake."

" And how did this demon come in ? "

" By the door, Juana, by the door."

4

" Without knocking! Without waiting to be let in ! "

" That is the devil's way," replied Berta's father; " he will slip in anywhere. I was not expecting him; I was reading that book that is lying open on the table, and as I was turning over a leaf, I felt something like a breath of air; I looked up and saw him before me. I was struck with amazement. I tried to rise, but he put his hand on my shoulder and obliged me to remain seated; and he smiled all the time; that is to say, he laughed in my face. He made a thousand excuses, indeed, treating me with such familiarity that before I had offered him a chair, he took one himself and sat down in it as if he had been in his own house."

Nurse Juana listened without moving a muscle of her face, and she would have thought that Berta's father was jesting if the terror depicted on his countenance had not testified to the truth of his words. Besides, the good man was not in the habit of jesting. Had he become suddenly mad? Mad, a man of so much good sense ! The nurse crossed herself, inwardly, without knowing what to think of what she had just heard.

" And who was he looking for ? " she asked; " what did he want? "

" He came in boldly," answered Berta's father. " He wanted me, and he came to make a proposal to me."

" A proposal ! " exclaimed Juana.

" Yes, that is what it was, a proposal. What do you suppose he wants ? "

" What ? "

" Oh !—"

" What is it ? "

" He wants—"

He stopped, as if he found it necessary to make a great effort, and clasping his hands he cried :

" He wants to marry Berta ! "

" To marry Berta ! " repeated Juana, crossing herself again.

" Just as you hear.—He came very frankly to ask me for her hand."

" And you rated him soundly for his presumption, and the poor devil went away with a *No* as big as a house."

" Ah, Nurse Juana, one does n't say no to the devil so easily as that. I was unable to resist him, I could not defend myself, and he has got my word. What shall I do now! He is young, handsome, and rich, he has a sweet voice, but he says some things that terrify one— What is to become of her ? No, I cannot reconcile myself to the thought of her marrying him. I have given my consent, but now I would say no to him a thousand times over — now, that he is not here ; for you must know that his presence ties the hands and binds the tongue."

"What a man!" cried the nurse in dismay.

Berta's father was very kind-hearted, and he had a very good opinion of mankind; thus it was that he shook his head despondently as he replied:

" A man!—A man would not be so cruel to me. To take Berta from me is to take my life. It is to assassinate me without allowing me a chance to defend myself; and that is the most horrible part of it—they will be married, and Berta will be united for life to the murderer of her father."

The nurse folded her arms and there was a moment of sorrowful silence.

Suddenly she said:

" Ah!—Berta will refuse."

A bitter smile crossed the lips of the unhappy father.

"You think she will not?" said the nurse. " Now, we shall see."

And she turned to go for Berta, but at the same moment the curtain was raised and Berta entered the room.

The red carnation glowed in her black hair like fire in the darkness; her eyes shone with a strange light, and in the fearless expression of her countenance was to be divined the strength of an unalterable resolution.

She looked alternately at her father and at her nurse, and then in a trembling voice she said:

" I know all. It may be to my life-long happiness ; it may be to my eternal misery ; but that man is the master of my heart."

She smiled first at her father and then at her nurse; and left the room with the same tranquillity with which she had entered it.

The nurse and the father remained standing where she left them, motionless, dumb, astounded.

The devil then had succeeded in gaining an entrance into Berta's house in the manner in which we have seen ; and not only had he gained an entrance into it, but he had taken possession of it as if it had always been his own. He was hardly out of it before he was back again. He spent in it several of his mornings, many of his afternoons, and all his evenings ; and there was no way of escaping his assiduous visits, for Berta was always there to receive him. And it was not easy to be angry with him, either; for he possessed the charm of an irresistible gayety, and one had not only to be resigned but to show pleasure at his constant presence. Besides, neither Berta's father nor the housekeeper dared to treat him coldly; they felt compelled, by what irresistible spell they knew not, to receive him with all honor and with a smiling countenance.

This is the case when they are under the influence of his presence: but when he is absent, the father and the nurse treat him without any ceremony whatever. The two get together in secret and in whispers revenge themselves upon him by picking him to pieces. In these secret backbitings they give vent to the aversion with which he inspires them ; and the father and the nurse between them leave him without a single good quality.

And it is not without reason that they berate him, for since he took the house by storm nothing is done in it but what pleases him ; he it is who rules it, he it is who orders everything. For Berta thinks that all he does is right, and there is no help for it but to bow in silence to her will.

But they are not satisfied with berating him ; they also conspire against him. What means shall they take to overthrow the power of this unlawful ruler ?—for in the eyes of the housekeeper he is a usurper, and in those of Berta's father, a tyrant;—turn him out of the house ? This is the one thought of the conspirators. But how ? This is the difficulty which confronts them.

Two means entirely opposed to each other occur to them—to fly from him or to make a stand against him. To fly is the plan of Berta's father ; it is the resource which is most consistent with his pacific character. To fly far from him, far away, to the ends of the earth.

But to this the housekeeper answers :

" Fly from him ! What nonsense ! Where could we go, that he would not follow us ? No ;

such folly is not to be thought of. What we ought to do is to take a firm stand and defend ourselves against him."

"Defend ourselves against him!" exclaimed Berta's father. "With what weapons? With what strength?"

"Neither strength nor weapons are required," replied the nurse. "Some day you bar the door against him, and then he may knock in vain. Satan turns away from closed doors."

"Nurse Juana, that is folly," replied Berta's father; "if he does not come in by the door he will come in by the window, or down the chimney."

Juana bit her lips reflectively, for what she had never been able to explain satisfactorily to herself was how he had succeeded in entering the house for the first time, for the door was always kept closed; it was necessary to knock to have it opened; and it was never opened unless under the inspection of the housekeeper; she always wanted to know who came in and who went out, and in this she was very particular. How then had he been able to come in without being seen or heard?

Her first inquiries on this mysterious point were addressed to Berta—and Berta answered simply that he had entered without knocking because the door was open. This the nurse found impossible to believe.

She remained thoughtful, then, for this demon of a man, it seemed, could in truth enter the house even if the door were barred.

The conspirators did not get beyond these two courses of action : to fly or to defend themselves. To fly was impossible, and to defend themselves was impracticable. Berta's father and the house-keeper discussed these two points daily without seeing light on any side. And must they resign themselves to living under the diabolical yoke of that man ? Both found themselves in a situation that would be difficult to describe. They lived in constant trepidation, fearing they knew not what.

And who, then, is this man who rules them with his presence and who has made himself master of Berta's heart ? His name is Adrian Baker, he lives alone, and he possesses a large fortune. This is all that is known about him.

For the rest, he is young, tall, graceful in fig-ure, with hair like gold and a complexion as fair as snow ; ardent and impassioned in speech, and with steadfast, searching, and melancholy eyes, blue as the blue of deep waters.

His manners could not be more natural, affec-tionate, and simple than they are. He enters the house and runs up the stairs, two steps at a time. Nothing stops him. If he meets Berta's father, he rushes to him and embraces him, and the good man trembles from head to foot in the pressure of those affectionate embraces. If it is the housekeeper who comes to meet him, he lays his hand affectionately on her shoulder, and he always has some pleasant remark to make, some cunning flattery which awakens in the nurse a strange emotion. She feels as if the sap of youth were, of a sudden, flowing through her veins.

There is no way of escaping the magic of his words, the spell of his voice, the charm of his presence. Juana has observed that when he looks at Berta his eyes shine with a light like that which the eyes of cats emit in the dark; she has observed also that Berta turns pale under the power of his glance, and that she bows her head under it as if yielding to the influence of an irresistible will.

She has observed still more : she has observed that this mysterious man at times sits lost in thought, his chin resting on his hand and a frown on his brows, as if he saw some dreadful vision before him, and that presently, as if awakening from a dream, he talks and smiles and laughs as before. Berta's father has observed, on his side, that he knows something about everything, understands something of everything, has an explanation for everything, comprehends and divines everything, as if he possessed the secret of all things. And these observations they communicate to each other, filled with wonder and amazement.

Sometimes, sitting beside Berta, he amuses himself winding the linen floss or the silks with which she is embroidering, or in cutting fantastic figures out of any scrap of paper that may be at hand. Then he is like a child. At other times he speaks of the world and of men, of foreign countries and of remote ages, with so much gravity and judgment that he seems like an old man who has retired from the world laden with wisdom and experience.

But when he seats himself at the piano, then one can only yield one's self unresistingly to the caprices of his will. The keys, touched by his fingers, produce melodies so sparkling, so joyous, that the soul is filled with gayety; but suddenly he changes to another key and the piano moans and sighs like a human voice, and the heart is moved and the eyes fill with tears. But this is not all; for, when one least expects it, thunder low and deep seems to roll through the instrument; and strains are heard, now near, now distant, that thrill the heart, and tones that fill the soul with terror; through the vibrating chords all the spirits of the other world seem to be speaking in an unknown tongue.

It is all very well for the housekeeper to regard Adrian Baker as the devil in person, or as a man possessed by the devil, or at least as an extraordinary being, who possesses the diabolical secret of some wonder-working philtre. It is all very well for Berta's father to see in him a masterful mind and an eccentric nature. And who knows —he has sometimes heard of mysterious fluids, of subtle forces which attract and repel, of dominating influences, of marvels of magnetism ; and although he has never given a great deal of thought to any of those matters, he thinks about them since he has felt himself dominated by this singular personage, and Adrian Baker has become, in fact, his fixed idea, his absorbing thought, his unceasing preoccupation, his constant monomania. Berta's father and the housekeeper may very well attribute to him marvellous powers, suggested by their own excited imaginations ; but we must not share in those hallucinations, nor are we to conclude from them that Adrian Baker is outside the common law to which ordinary mortals are subject.

This is evident; but, still, who is Adrian Baker ?

We shall present here all the information that we have been able to gather about him, and let each one draw from it the conclusion he pleases.

It is not yet quite two years since one of the carriages which transport passengers from the railway station to the city which is the scene of our story, drove rapidly from the station ; the energy with which the coachman whipped up his horses showed the haste or the importance of the travellers it carried.

This carriage entered the city and stopped before the door of the best hotel of the place; there the solitary traveller it carried alighted from it, and this traveller was Adrian Baker. He was enveloped in a travelling great-coat lined with costly fur. The eagerness with which the waiters of the hotel hastened to meet him showed that they had discovered in the new guest a mine of tips. The coachman took his leave of him, hat in hand, and as he turned away looked around at the bystanders, displaying to them a gold coin in his left eye.

Nothing more was needed to cause the luggage of the guest to be whisked off to the most sumptuous room in the hotel. Seven cities of Greece disputed with one another the honor of having been the birthplace of Homer; more than seven waiters disputed with one another the honor of carrying Adrian Baker's valise. He was like a king entering his palace.

For several days he was to be seen alone and on foot, traversing the streets and visiting the most noteworthy buildings; then, alone also, but in a carriage, he was to be seen viewing the wildest and most picturesque spots in the neighborhood, with the attention of an artist, a philosopher, or a poet.

He was affable and easy in his manners; and

he soon had many friends who talked admiringly of his eccentricities, of his riches, and of his learning ; so that he was for some time the lion of the day, and therefore the favorite subject of every conversation. To win his friendship would have been for the men a triumph ; and to win his heart would have been for the haughtiest woman more than a triumph ; but Adrian Baker kept his inmost heart closed alike to friendship and to love ; so that only three things were known about him—that he was young, that he was rich, and that he had travelled over half the world.

He was supposed to be an Englishman, a German, or an American ; in the first place, because he was fair, and in the second place, because, although he spoke Spanish as if it were his native tongue, a certain foreign flavor was to be noticed in his accent, which each one interpreted according to his fancy.

For the rest, he seemed pleased with the beauty of the sky and the gayety of the landscape, and although he had told no one whether he intended to remain there long or not, the fact was that he did not go away. Doubtless he grew tired of the life at the hotel, for one day he suddenly bought a fine house and established himself in it like a prince. This edifice, venerable from its antiquity, had the grandiose aspect of a palace, and one of its angles fronted Berta's house.

This is all that was known about Adrian Baker.

We now know, therefore, that the mysterious Adrian Baker was neither more nor less than Berta's neighbor himself.

One night, returning from his daily visit to Berta, he entered the house, crossed the hall, and shut himself up in his own apartments. Shortly afterwards the great door of the palace, creaking harshly on its hinges, was closed; the lights were extinguished one by one, and everything remained in profound silence. Adrian Baker, however, was not asleep.

At the further end of the room, which was lighted by the soft light of a lamp, he sat with his elbows resting on a mahogany table and his face buried in his hands, seemingly lost in thought. And his thoughts could not be of a pleasant nature, for the stern frown upon his brow showed that some storm was raging behind that forehead smooth as a child's and pale as death. The light of the lamp, reflected from his golden hair, seemed to envelop his head in fantastic lights and shadows.

After many moments of immobility and silence, he struck the table violently with the palm of his hand, exclaiming :

" Accursed riches !   Odious learning !   Cruel experience ! "

Then he rose to his feet, and striding up and down the room like a madman, he cried in smothered accents :

"Faith ! Faith ! Doubt is killing me ! "

A moment later he shook his beautiful head and burst into a terrible laugh.

" Very well," he said. " The proof is a terrible one, but I require this proof. I must descend into the tomb to obtain it : well, then, I will descend into the tomb. I must consult the sombre oracle of death concerning the mysteries of life : well, then, I will consult it."

At this moment the glass chimney of the lamp burst, falling to the floor in a thousand fragments ; the lurid flame sent forth a black smoke that filled the room with shadows which crept along the walls, mingled together on the ceiling, and crossed one another on the floor ; the furniture seemed to be moving, the ceiling sinking down, and the walls receding.

In the midst of this demon dance of lights and shadows, the flame of the lamp went out, as if in obedience to an invisible breath, and in the darkness that followed all was silence. .

Something extraordinary must have occurred in Berta's house, for the nurse seemed to have been seized by a sudden fit of restlessness that would not let her sit still for a moment. She went to and fro, upstairs and down, out and in, with the mechanical movement of an automaton. It was a sort of nervous attack that had in a moment increased twofold the housekeeper's domestic activity. Suddenly she would stand still, and placing her forefinger on her upper lip she would remain motionless, as if she were seeking in her mind the explanation of some mystery or the key to some riddle, gesticulating with expressive eloquence, and, so to say, thinking in gestures.

But the cause of the agitation which we observe in her could not be a very alarming one, for in the midst of it all there was apparent something like joy, a secret joy which in spite of herself was perceptible through her restlessness and her gesticulations. In our poor human nature, joy and sorrow often manifest themselves by the same symptoms; and a piece of good news will agitate us in the same way as a piece of bad news.

Be this as it may, what is certain is that the housekeeper seemed to be excited by some secret thought which she turned over and over in her mind, and that she was waiting for something with impatience, for from time to time she stood still, stretched out her neck, and listened.

Suddenly the door-bell rang twice; slowly, deliberately, producing on the nurse the effect of an electric shock. She threw down some house-linen which she had in her hands, overturned a chair or two that stood in her way, and tore a curtain that opposed her progress, leaving devastation and destruction in her wake, like a storm.

She pulled the cord which opened the door, and she pulled it so violently that the door sprang wide open, giving admittance to Berta's father, who entered slowly, leaning on his cane like a man whose vitality is beginning to fail. As he entered, he raised his eyes with a look of melancholy discouragement, and at the head of the stairs he saw the housekeeper, who seemed to be trying to tell him something, gesticulating violently and waving her arms like the apparatus of a semaphore. The good man did not understand a word of this telegraphic language, and he stopped at the foot of the stairs, endeavoring to comprehend the meaning of the signs which the housekeeper was excitedly making above his head. But, naturally, he was not very skilful in this kind of investigation, and his not very vivid imagination was at this moment paralyzed. Finally, he shrugged his shoulders with a sort of resigned and patient desperation, as if to say, "What are you trying to tell me?" The housekeeper folded her arms and shook her head three times; this meant: "Stupid! stupid! stupid!" The good man bent his head under the triple accusation, and proceeded to ascend the stairs. At the head Nurse Juana was waiting for him, and without further ceremony she took him by the hand and drew him into his room; and there, after assuring herself that no one was within hearing, she put her mouth close

5

to the ear of Berta's father, and in a mysterious voice, and with an air of profound mystery, she said to him:

"He is going away!"

"He is going away!" repeated Berta's father, exhaling a profound sigh.

"Yes," she added; "we are going to be free."

"Free!" repeated the good man, shaking his head with an air of incredulity. Then he asked:

"And where is he going?"

"He is going very far away," answered the nurse. "That is certain. He is going very far away, to some place, I don't know where, at the other end of the earth. It is a sudden journey."

The good man sighed again despondently; Nurse Juana looked at him with amazement, saying:

"Any one would suppose that I had just given you a piece of bad news. Can that man have bewitched you to the extent—"

"Yes," he interrupted, "for if he goes he will not go alone; he will take Berta with him, and then what is to become of us?"

"Nothing of the kind," replied Juana. "He will go alone—entirely alone."

"Worse and worse," said the father, "for then, what is to become of Berta?"

"Nothing," said the nurse. "Out of sight, out

of mind. The absent are forgotten; the dead
are buried. That is the way of the world. Berta
knows all about it; she told me herself, and she
is as calm and as cool as possible. Bah, she
won't need any cordial to keep her up when she
is bidding him good-bye."

As she uttered the last word she turned her
head and she could not restrain the cry that
rose to her lips as she saw Adrian Baker, who
had just entered—Adrian Baker, in person, paler
than ever, dressed in a handsome travelling suit.
His eyes shone with a strange lustre, and a smile,
half sad, half mocking, curved his lips.

He begged a thousand pardons for the surprise which he had caused them, and said that
unforeseen circumstances obliged him to under-
take a sudden journey to New York, where he
was urgently called by affairs of the greatest importance, but that he would return soon.

"I am going away," he ended, "but I leave
my heart here and I will come back for it."

Saying this, he embraced Berta's father so
affectionately that the worthy man was deeply
moved, and Nurse Juana, dominated by the
voice and the presence of this singular man, felt
a tear or two spring to her eyes, which she hastened to wipe away with the corner of her apron.

Adrian Baker laid his hand on her shoulder,
a hand which the nurse felt tremble, and she
trembled herself as she heard him say:

" That is the way of the world, eh ?   Well, we shall see."

Then he left the room, and the father and the nnrse followed him mechanically.

Berta came out to meet them, and her hand sought Adrian Baker's, and both hands remained clasped for a long time.

" You will come back soon ? " asked Berta, in soft and trembling accents.

" Soon," he answered.

" When ? " she asked.

" Soon," repeated Baker.   " If you wait for me your heart will announce my return to you."

" I will wait for ever for you," said Berta, in a choking voice, but without a tear in her eyes.

Their hands unclasped, Adrian Baker hurried to the stairs, ran down precipitately, and shortly afterward they heard the rolling of the carriage which bore him away.

Bertha gave her father a gentle smile and then ran to shut herself up in her room.

As the noise of the carriage wheels died away in the distance, like a dying peal of thunder, the housekeeper crossed herself, and said :

" He is gone ; now we can breathe freely."

Apparently Nurse Juana knew the human heart well, or at least Berta's heart, for three months had passed since Adrian Baker had sailed for New York, and not once had she been able to surprise a tear in the eyes of the girl to whom she had taken the place of a mother. Berta apparently felt no grief at his absence.

It is true that during these three months of absence a letter had been received from New York, in which Adrian Baker said to Berta all that is said in such cases ; it was a simple, tender and earnest letter, that did not seem to have been written three thousand miles away ; on the other side of the great ocean in which the most ardent and the most profound passions are wrecked. It is true that this letter was answered by return of mail, and that it traversed the stormy solitudes of the sea full of promises and hopes.

It is also true that Berta put away Adrian Baker's letter carefully, treasuring it as one treasures a relic. It is true that she passed whole hours seated at her piano running her fingers up and down the keys, playing Adrian Baker's favorite airs, which he himself had taught her. But except this, Berta lived like other girls ; she had an excellent appetite and she slept the tranquil sleep of a happy heart. She spent the usual time at her toilet table and she took pleasure in making herself beautiful. Some of the asperities of her character had become softened ; she spoke with all her natural vivacity, and, finally, she never mentioned Adrian Baker's name.

Her father and her nurse observed all this and deduced as a consequence that the traveller had left no trace in Berta's heart. Only one fear troubled them,—the fear that he would return.

In this way another month passed, and the memory of Adrian Baker began to wear away; if his name was sometimes mentioned, it was as one evokes the memory of a dream.

The dream, however, at times assumed the aspect of an impending reality. He might return, and beyond a doubt he had not intended to remain away for ever; his last farewell had not been an eternal one. If he himself was on the other side of the ocean, three thousand miles away, that is, in New York, at the other end of the earth, more, in the other world, his house was there, opposite them, open, kept by his servants with the same luxury and the same pomp as before he had gone away ; his house that seemed like an enchanted palace waiting for its owner ; and the order and care with which everything was conducted in it indicated that the servants did not wish to be surprised by the sudden appearance of their master ; that is to say, that Adrian Baker might return at any moment. The plants on the terrace spread their branches as full of life as if they were tended by the hands of Adrian Baker himself.

Berta's father and the housekeeper saw in this house a constant menace ; it came to be for them the shadow, so to say, of Adrian Baker ; but for all that, time passed and the traveller did not return.

Spring came, and nature bloomed again with all the richness of vegetation which she displays in southern climes; and it is in the heart of the South that the scene of our story is laid. Everything put on its fairest and most smiling aspect, and the soul felt the vague happiness of a hope that is about to be realized.

Berta shared in this beautiful awakening of nature, and it might be said that her every beauty had acquired a new charm; her eyes seemed larger, her glance gentler, calmer, more profound; her cheeks fresher, softer, and rosier; and her smile more tender, innocent, and enchanting. Her figure had acquired a majestic ease, which gave to her movements voluptuousness and firmness. It seemed as if youth had made a supreme effort, and in giving the last touch to her beauty had obtained a masterpiece. She was in the full splendor of her loveliness.

In exchange, Adrian Baker's palace one morning appeared as gloomy as a sepulchre; the drawn blinds and the closed hall-door gave it the aspect of a deserted house; profound silence reigned within it, and yet the palace of Adrian Baker was still inhabited.

In the hall the figure of the porter appeared like a shade; he was dressed entirely in black, and all the other servants of the house were also clad in mourning, and in their faces were to be observed signs of sadness.

What had happened ?

What had happened was simply that Adrian Baker had died in New York of an acute attack of pneumonia. The news had spread through the city with the rapidity with which bad news spreads, and it had also penetrated into Berta's house. At first it seemed incredible that Adrian Baker should have died, as if the life of this man were not subject to the contingencies to which the lives of other mortals are subject. But the tidings had been confirmed and they must be believed. Besides, the aspect of the palace bore testimony to the authenticity of the news. In that house hung with black the very stones seemed to mourn. The news had come in a black-bordered letter dated in New York and signed by the head of the house of Wilson and Company, with which Adrian Baker had large sums deposited.

Berta's father and the housekeeper looked at each other with amazement, and repeated, one after the other :

" He is dead ! "

" He is dead ! "

Berta, pale as death itself, surprised them as they uttered these words, and in a sepulchral voice she said :

" Yes, he has died in New York, but he lives in my heart."

And turning from them she fled to her room

and seated herself at the window from which she could see the terrace of the palace. The flowers, agitated gently by the breezes of spring, leaned toward Berta as if sending her a melancholy greeting. She gazed at them without a tear in her eyes. The extreme pallor of her face and the slight trembling of her lips alone revealed the grief that afflicted her soul.

Suddenly the flight of a white butterfly circling in the air attracted her gaze. She followed it absently with her eyes, and the butterfly, as if drawn by Berta's gaze, tracing capricious circles, left the terrace, flew swiftly to Berta's window and entered the room.

With an involuntary movement Berta extended her hands to catch it, but the butterfly darted between them, and circled swiftly and silently about her head, forming around her brow a sort of aureole, which appeared and disappeared like a succession of lightning flashes. The wings of the butterfly glowed above Bertha's head with a light like the first splendors of the dawn. Then it passed before her eyes, she saw it hovering over the flowers on the terrace, and then it disappeared from her gaze as if it had vanished into air. Her eyes sought it with indescribable eagerness, but in vain; she saw it no more.

She clasped her hands and two large tears rose to her eyes and rolled down her cheeks.

On the following day the housekeeper, enter-ing Berta's room, saw a shadow outlined against the wall above the head of her bed. This shadow, as the nurse looked, took the form of a human head.

It was the head of Adrian Baker, the same head, with its pale forehead, its compelling glance, and its smile, at once sweet, sad, and mocking.

The housekeeper, out of her wits with terror, crossed herself as if she had seen a diabolical vision and hurried out of the room.

Adrian Baker's death has wrought terrible ravages in Berta. She does not distress those around her by ceaseless sighs and tears; she does not continually proclaim in words the depth of her sorrow; on the contrary, she hides her grief in her own breast, devours her tears in secret, chokes back her sighs and utters no un-availing complaints; Adrian Baker's name is never heard from her lips.

It might be thought that she had consoled her-self easily, if in her eyes there did not lie the shadow of a deep grief, if the pallor of her cheeks did not cover her youthful beauty like a funeral pall, if her hollow voice did not reveal the profound loneliness of her heart. At times she smiles at her father, but in her smiles there is an inexpressible bitterness. She can be seen fading away, like the flame of an expiring lamp. Like a miser she hides her grief in the bottom of her heart, as if she feared that it might be taken from her.

Her father and her nurse see her growing thin, they see her fading away, they see her dying, without being able to stop the ravages of the persistent, voiceless, inconsolable grief that is slowly sapping her youth and her life, and they curse the name of Adrian Baker, and they would at the same time give their lives to bring him back to life; but death does not give up its prey, and only one hope remains to them, the last hope—time.

But time passes, and the memory of Adrian Baker, like a slow poison, is gradually consuming Berta's life.

Everything has been done : she has been surrounded with all the delights of the world ; the most eligible suitors have sued for her favor; youth, beauty, and wealth have disputed her affection with one another, but her grief has remained inaccessible; she has been subjected to every proof, but it has not been possible to tear from her soul the demon image of Adrian Baker. Medical skill has been appealed to, and science has exhausted its resources in vain, for Berta's malady is incurable.

The nurse firmly believes that Adrian Baker has bewitched her ; he has diffused through her

blood a diabolical philtre. Strong love will survive absence, but no love will survive death.
Berta, consequently, was bewitched.

Her father has only one thought, expressed in
these words : " He has gone away and he is taking her with him ; after all, he is taking her with
him."

But there is still one other resource to be appealed to—solitude, the fields, nature. Who can
tell ! the sky, the sun, the air of the country, may
revive her ; the poetry of nature may awaken in
her heart new feelings and new hopes ; the murmur of the waters, the song of the birds, the shade
of the trees—why not ? There is no human sorrow, however great it may be, that does not sink
into insignificance before the grandeur of the
heavens.

At a little distance from the city Berta's father
has a small villa, whose white walls and red roof
can be seen through the trees which surround it.
There could not be a more picturesque situation.
To the right, the mountain ; to the left, the plain ;
in front, the sea, stretching far in the distance,
until it blends with the horizon ; and that nothing
may be wanting to complete the picture, the ruins
of an ancient monastery, seated on the slope of
the mountain, can be seen from the villa.

Berta offered no resistance, for it was a matter
of indifference to her whether she lived in the
city or in the country ; the only thing she showed

any desire about was that the piano should be taken with them, as if she regarded it as a dear friend and her only confidant; and the family removed to the villa and established themselves in it.

Berta herself arranged the room which she was to occupy in the villa. This opened on the garden and served her both as bedroom and dressing-room. Above her bed she hung a beautiful life-size photograph of a head. It was that of Adrian Baker, with his pale, smooth brow, his large blue eyes and his beautiful golden curls—the head of Adrian Baker admirably photographed, and which she herself had shaded.

For the piano no place could be found to please Berta. There was only one common room in the villa, the parlor, which at times also served as a dining-room. She was hesitating between the parlor and her bedroom, when the idea occurred to her to put it in a small pavilion covered with vines and honeysuckles, which stood in a corner of the garden and which was used as a hot-house. The idea seemed to be a happy one, and she smiled as it occurred to her, and the piano was placed in the pavilion, like a bird in its cage.

The journey must have fatigued Berta, for she retired early to her room, where the nurse left her in bed. Did she sleep? We cannot say; but at dawn the songs of the birds that made their nests in the garden caused her to rise. She

opened the window-shutters and a flock of birds
flew away frightened, to hide themselves in the
tops of the trees, gilded by the first rays of the
sun.   Before long, however, the boldest of them
returned to hop before her window, looking at
Berta with a certain audacious familiarity as if
they recognized in her an old friend.   A few
grains of wheat and a few crumbs of bread scattered on the window-sill gradually attracted the
more timid, who grew at last to be familiar.   The
slightest movement, indeed, caused them to take
flight precipitately ; but they soon recovered their
lost confidence and they returned again to hop
gayly on the iron railing of the window.

Berta watched them, and as she watched them
she smiled ; and at the end of a few days she had
induced them to come in and out with perfect
confidence.   In her solitary walks through the
garden and through the avenue of lime trees
which led to the villa, they followed her, flying
from tree to tree.   She spent a few hours of the
morning, every day, in the pavilion, and there
the birds came also, mingling their joyous carols
with the melancholy strains of the piano ; but the
mad gayety of the birds was powerless to mitigate
the profound sadness of Berta ; her one thought
was still Adrian—Adrian Baker.

This name, which never escaped her lips, was
to be seen written everywhere by Berta's hand,
on the garden walls, on the trunks of the trees ;

and even the vines that covered the pavilion had interlaced their branches in such a manner that "Adrian Baker" could be deciphered in them. This name was to be met everywhere, like the mute echo of an undying memory.

During the morning hours Berta's countenance seemed to be more animated, and her cheeks had even at times a rosy hue; but as the day declined her transient animation faded away, as if the sun of her life too approached its setting.

Seated at her window she contemplated in silence the clouds illumined by the last rays of the setting sun. Juana, who had exhausted in vain all her subjects of conversation, was with her. A sudden brightness hovered over Berta's head for an instant, circled swiftly around it, and then vanished from sight.

"Did you see it?" cried Berta.

"Yes," answered the nurse, "it was a white butterfly that wanted to settle on your head."

"Well?" asked Berta.

"White butterflies," said the nurse, "are a sign of good luck; they always bring good news."

"Yes," answered Berta, pressing her nurse's hand convulsively. "That is my white butterfly, and this time it will not deceive me. Adrian is coming—yes, he is coming for me; that is what it has come to tell me—I was waiting for it."

The nurse gazed at her for a moment with dilated eyes; the setting sun illumined Berta's countenance with a strange light, and the poor woman, unable to support the look which burned in the eyes of the sick girl, bent her head and clasped her hands, saying to herself :

" My God ! She has lost her mind ! "

The idea that Berta had lost her reason threw the housekeeper into a state of distraction. She would hide herself in the remotest corners of the house to cry by herself. She could not bear alone the burden of so terrible a secret, but to whom could she confide it ? How stab the father's heart so cruelly ! To tell him that Berta had lost her reason would be to kill him. The good man watched over his daughter with the eyes of love, but love itself made him blind and he did not perceive her madness.

And the housekeeper became every day more and more convinced of the reality of this dreadful misfortune. During the night she stole many times to the sleeping girl's bedside and listened to her calm breathing. No extraordinary change, either in her habits, or her acts, or her words, gave evidence of the wandering of her mind. True ; but she was waiting for Adrian Baker and she declared that he would come. It was in vain she tried to persuade her that this was folly, for Berta either grew angry and commanded her to be silent, or smiled with scornful pity at her arguments. Was not this madness ?

The housekeeper suddenly lost her appetite and her sleep; and she shunned Berta's father, for she was not sure of being able to keep the secret which she carried in her bosom. The same thought kept revolving in her mind like a mill. It seemed as if Berta's madness was going to cost the nurse also her reason.

One night she lay tossing about, unable to sleep, her imagination filled with dreadful spectres. In the midst of the darkness she saw faces approaching and receding from her, that laughed and wept, that vanished to appear again, and all these faces that danced before her eyes had, notwithstanding their grotesque features, a diabolical likeness to the head of Adrian Baker. The nurse, terrified, shut her eyes, that she might not see them, but notwithstanding she still continued seeing them.

She thought that she was under the influence of a nightmare, and making an effort she sat up in the bed. Suddenly she heard a distant sound of sweet music, a mysterious melody whose notes died away on the breeze.

She listened attentively, and she soon comprehended that the music she heard came from the piano; and she sprang out of bed, crying:

" Berta ! Berta ! "

She began to dress herself quickly, groping for her things in the darkness, saying as she did so, in a voice full of anguish:

6

"Alone, in the pavilion, and at this hour! Child of my heart, you are mad!"

All the visions she had seen disappeared; she saw nothing, she only heard the distant notes of the piano breaking the silence of the night.

Going into the hall she groped her way to Berta's room. She gently pushed in the door, which opened noiselessly, and an indistinct glimmer, like the last gleam of twilight, met her eyes. It was the light of the night-lamp burning softly in its porcelain vase.

Her first glance was at the bed, which, in the indistinct light, presented to her eyes only a shapeless object; but in a moment more she saw that the bed was empty.

She thought of taking the lamp that burned in the corner of the room to light her way and going to the pavilion, but at this moment she felt a breath of cold damp air blowing softly on her face.

She turned her eyes in the direction from which the breeze had come, and observed that the window was wide open and that outside all was profound darkness.

And filled with indescribable amazement, unwilling to believe the evidence of her eyes, she saw what appeared to be a human figure standing motionless in front of the window, its hands clasped and its forehead resting against the window-frame.

A cold perspiration, like that of death, broke out over her; she would have shuddered, but she could not; she attempted to cry out, but her voice died away in her throat; she attempted to fly, but her feet, fastened to the ground, refused to carry her.

With her eyes starting from their sockets, her mouth wide open, and terror depicted on her countenance, she stood as if petrified, without the strength to keep erect or the will to fall.

And in truth she had some reason to be terrified.

Before her stood Berta, leaning motionless against the window, drinking in with rapt attention the notes which at that moment came in a torrent from the piano.

It was not Berta, then, who was breaking the silence of the night with that mysterious music.

What unknown hand, what invisible hand was it that drew those sounds from the chords of the piano in the midst of the silence and the solitude of the night! Was what her eyes saw real! Was what her ears were listening to real! Or was it all the dreadful hallucination of a terrible dream!

And this was not all; for the memory of the terrified nurse recalls with a secret shudder those mysterious melodies which now enchain her ear. Yes; through the piano roll sounds like the rumbling of thunder, and strains are heard, now near, now far, that thrill the heart, and tones that fill the soul with terror; through the vibrating chords all the spirits of the other world seem to be speaking in an unknown tongue.

I do not know how long the housekeeper might have stood silent and motionless, under the influence of the terror which mastered her, if Berta had not observed her.

It caused her neither surprise nor alarm to see her nurse there. Approaching her she took her by the hand, and, shaking her gently, said:

"Do you see?—Do you hear?—It is Adrian— Adrian who has come for me; the white butterfly did not deceive me."

The housekeeper had by this time recovered herself sufficiently to pass her hand over her forehead and to rub her eyes.

"I knew that he would come," continued Berta; "I have been waiting for him every day."

The nurse, as if by a supreme effort, drew a deep breath.

"Do you hear those sighs that come from the piano?" said Berta. "It is he; he is calling me; and since you are here, let us go to meet him."

And taking the lamp in her hand as she spoke, she added:

"Follow me."

Nurse Juana followed her like a ghost.

They entered the garden and walked toward

the pavilion. The pale light of the lamp illumined Berta's countenance, shedding around it
a fantastic light that made the surrounding darkness seem more intense.

The nurse felt herself drawn along by Berta;
she walked mechanically; a power stronger than
her terror impelled her.

In this way they crossed the garden and
reached the door of the pavilion. There Berta
stopped, and called softly:

"Adrian!"

But there was no response to her call.

Then they entered the pavilion.

Juana caught hold of Berta to keep from falling, and closed her eyes

The light of the lamp illumined the pavilion,
whose solitude seemed startled by this unexpected
visit; the piano was open and mute.

"No one!" exclaimed Berta, sighing.

"No one," repeated Juana, opening her eyes.

And so it was; the pavilion was empty.

It is beyond a doubt that Berta's piano has
the marvellous quality of making its strings sound
without the intervention of the human hand. And
this being the case, it must be admitted that
this marvellous instrument is, in addition, a con-
summate musician, for it plays with the skill at-
tained only by great artists.

But since Nurse Juana cannot conceive how a

piano can play of itself, without a hand moving
the keys, she has decided that in this diabolical
affair an invisible hand, the ghostly hand of some
spirit from the other world, has intervened.

This supposition is not altogether admissible,
for it seems to have been sufficiently proved that
spirits do not possess hands.   But the nurse does
not stop for such fine distinctions, and she firmly
believes that the spirit of Adrian Baker is wandering about the villa.   Condemned perhaps to
eternal torment, he takes pleasure in torturing
the living even after his death.

And it is indeed a diabolical amusement, for
the serenade is repeated nightly ; the family are
aroused from sleep ; they hasten to the pavilion
and the piano becomes silent ; they enter it and
they find no one.   They have observed that the
airs played by Berta in the morning are repeated
by the piano at night.

Juana is assailed by continual terrors ; there
is no peace in the house.   Berta's father is unable to explain the mystery, and his mind is filled
with confusion and his heart is a prey to sudden
alarms.   The light of day dissipates the agitation
of their minds, they fancy themselves the victims
of vain hallucinations, and, arming themselves
with heroic valor, they make plans for unravelling
the awesome mystery.

The most courageous among them would hide
in the pavilion, and there await in concealment

the hour of the strange occurrence; in this way they would discover what fingers drew those sounds from the piano.

Strong in this purpose they awaited the first shades of night; but then the courage of the strongest failed. The air became filled with fearful shadows, the silence with mysterious noises, and no one ventured to leave the house. They spent the nights in vigil and the terror by which all were possessed made them seem interminable.

And for Berta, on the other hand, the days were interminable, and she awaited the nights with eager impatience.

One afternoon she expressed a desire to visit the ruins of the monastery, and she showed so much eagerness in the matter that there was no resource but to accede to her wish. Her father and her nurse resolved to accompany her, and the three set out.

The distance between the villa and the monastery was not great, but the party walked slowly. In the winding path the ruins disappeared suddenly behind a hill, as if the earth had swallowed them; a few steps further on they suddenly reappeared; and the travellers stood before the ruined portico.

From this point the eye could contemplate the ruined walls, the broken partitions, the ceilings fallen in, and between the loose stones the solitary flowers of the ruin. Only the arches which supported the vaulted roof of the chapel had resisted the corroding influence of time.

The nurse would have now willingly returned to the villa, and Berta's father had no desire to go any further; but Berta passed through the ruined portico, and they were obliged to follow her.

She made her way into the chapel, passing under the crumbling arches which threatened at every moment to fall down and crush her, and she emerged at what must have been the centre of the monastery; for the remains of the wall and some broken and unsteady pilasters showed four paths which, uniting at their extremities, formed a square. This must have been the cloister; in the middle were vestiges of a choked-up cistern.

Here Berta sat down on a piece of cornice which was imbedded in the rubbish. She seemed pleased in the midst of this desolation. Her father and the nurse joined her with terror depicted on their countenances; they had heard the noise of footsteps in the chapel; more, Juana had seen a shadow glide away; how or where she did not know, but she was sure that she had seen it.

Berta smiled and said :

" The noise of footsteps and a shadow? Very well; what harm can those footsteps or that shadow do us ? They are perhaps the footsteps of Adrian Baker following us; it is his shade that accompanies us. What is there strange in that? Do you not know that I carry him in my heart? Do you not know that I am waiting for him, that I am always waiting for him?"

At the name of Adrian Baker, Berta's father and the nurse shuddered.

"Yes, my child," said the former, "but we are far from the villa, the sun is setting—it is growing late."

"Yes, yes," said Juana, "let us go back."

Berta drew her father affectionately toward her and said:

"Dear father, I am not mad. Juana, I am not mad. Adrian promised me that he would return, and he will return. I am waiting for him. Why should that be madness? I know that I grieve you, and I do not wish to grieve you. I have begged God a thousand times on my knees to tear his image from my heart and his memory from my mind; but God, who sees all things, from whom nothing is hidden, to whom all things are possible, has not wished to do it. Why? He alone knows."

The father's eyes filled with tears, and the nurse hid her face in her hands to keep back the sobs that rose in her throat.

Berta continued:

"Yes, it is growing late. But I am very tired. Let us wait a moment."

They had nothing to say in answer to her words, nor could they have said anything, for their voices failed them.

All three remained silent.

Suddenly they looked at one another with indescribable anxiety, for all three had heard a sigh, a human sigh that seemed exhaled by the ruins around them.

Could it have been the wind, moaning as it swept through the sharp points of the broken walls ?

Berta rose to her feet, and cried twice in a loud voice :

" Adrian ! Adrian !"

Her voice was borne away on the breeze, losing itself in the distance. But before the last notes died away, another voice resounded among the ruins, saying :

" Berta ! Berta !"

The sun had just set, and the twilight shadows gathered swiftly, as if they had sprung up from among the ruins, hiding the broken pillars and the crumbling walls.

In one of the angles of the cloister appeared a moving shadow. This shadow advanced slowly until it reached the middle of the court where the remains of the disused cistern were seen. There it stopped, and in a soft clear voice uttered the words :

" It is I, Berta ; it is I."

"He!" she cried, extending her arms in the air.

Juana uttered a cry of terror and caught hold of Berta with all the strength left her; the father tried to rise, but, unable to sustain himself, fell on his knees beside his daughter.

It was not possible to reject the evidence of their senses. Whatever might be the hidden cause of the marvel, the dark key of the mystery, the shadow which had just appeared in the angle of the cloister was clearly the authentic image, the *vera effigies*, the very person of Adrian Baker. The astonished eyes of Berta, of her father, and of the nurse could not refuse to believe it.

His fair curls, his pale brow, the outlines of his figure, his air, his glance, his voice—all were there before the amazed eyes of Berta, her father, and the nurse.

Now, was this a fantastic creation of their troubled senses? Was it a phantom of the brain, or a reality? Did all three suffer at the same time the same hallucination? The fixed thought of all three was Adrian Baker—and the senses often counterfeit the reality of our vain imaginings. The state of their minds, the place, the hour—and then, the air produces sounds that deceive; the light and the darkness mingling together in the mysterious hour of twilight people the solitude with strange visions. And in

the midst of those ruins, which began to assume
fantastic forms, and which seemed to move, in
the gathering shades of twilight, Berta, her father,
and the nurse might well believe themselves in
the presence of a spectre evoked there by their
presence.

But the fact was, that the shadow, instead of
vanishing, instead of changing its shape, as hap-
pens with chimeras of the brain, assumed before
their eyes a more distinct form, more definite
outlines, according as he approached the group.

Reaching them, he took gently in his the hands
Berta held out to him. His eyes shone with the
light of a supreme triumph.

"It is I," he said, in a moved voice. "I,
Adrian Baker. I am not a spectre risen from the
tomb."

Berta felt herself growing faint and was obliged
to sit down; and Adrian Baker continued thus:

"Forgive me. I have put your heart to a terrible proof, but the doubts of my soul were still
more terrible. The world had filled my spirit
with horrible distrust and I desired to sound the
uttermost depths of your love. It has resisted
absence, and it has resisted death. Your love
for me was not a passing fancy; you did not deceive yourself when you vowed me an eternal
love. I left you in order to watch you and I died
to comprehend you. I have followed you everywhere; I have not separated from you a single

moment. My sweet Berta! You waited for me living, and you have waited for me dead. 'If you wait for me,' I said, 'your own heart will announce my return to you,' and you see I have returned. I felt for you an immense tenderness, but a terrible doubt consumed my heart. Had my riches dazzled you? Forgive me, Berta. A fatal learning had frozen faith in my soul; I doubted everything, and I doubted your heart also—I doubted you."

Berta clasped her hands, and raising her eyes to heaven, exclaimed mournfully:

"My God! what cruel injustice!"

"Yes!" burst out Adrian Baker; "cruel injustice! but you have resuscitated my heart; you have brought my soul back to life."

"Ah," said Berta, laying her hands on his breast, "what if it were too late!"

Then, turning to her father and the nurse, she said:

"I feel very cold; let us return to the villa;" and leaning on Adrian Baker's arm, she led the way.

Her father and the nurse followed her in silence. The good man had comprehended everything, but the poor woman comprehended nothing.

What passed that night in the villa it is not necessary to relate; it was a night of pain, of agitation, and of anguish. It was necessary to go

to the city for a physician; why? Because Berta
was dying. Adrian Baker was the image of despair; the unhappy father wept as if his heart
would break, and the nurse stole away from time to
time to cry, unable to restrain her tears.

At dawn it was necessary to go again to the
city, for the physician of the body had exhausted
the resources of science, and they were obliged
to have recourse to the physician of the soul.

Dawn was just breaking when a priest alighted
at the door of the villa. The sick girl received
him, if we may be allowed the expression, with
melancholy gladness, and a little later all was
over.

In the middle of the room, on a funeral bier,
lighted by six large wax tapers, which cast a
melancholy light around, lay the body of the
dead girl. The window admitted the morning
light; and the autumn wind, tearing the dead
leaves from the trees in the garden, scattered
them over the inanimate form of Berta, as if
death thus rendered homage to death.

Attracted by the light of the torches, a white
butterfly flew silently in and circled around and
around the head of the dead girl.

Watching the body were the father, leaning over
the bier, bowed down under the weight of an im-
measurable grief; the nurse dissolved in tears;
Adrian, with dry and glittering eyes, pale, motionless, mute, terrible in his anguish; and the

priest with folded arms and head bent over his breast, murmuring pious prayers.

Such was the scene which the morning sun lighted in Berta's room. The birds of the garden alighted on the rail of the window, but did not venture to enter; they looked in apprehensively and flew away terrified; they twittered on the branches of the trees, and their melancholy chirpings seemed like sighs.

Breathing a sigh torn from the inmost depths of his soul, Adrian Baker exclaimed in a hollow voice:

"Miserable man that I am! I have killed her!"

"Ah, yes," said the priest, slowly shaking his head. "Divine Justice—Doubt kills."

MAESE PERÉZ, THE ORGANIST

BY

GUSTAVO ADOLFO BECQUER

From " Modern Ghosts." Translated by Rollo Ogden.

MAESE PÉREZ, THE ORGANIST

BY GUSTAVO ADOLFO BECQUER

I.

"DO you see that man with the scarlet cloak, and the white plume in his hat, and the gold-embroidered vest? I mean the one just getting out of his litter and going to greet that lady—the one coming along after those four pages who are carrying torches? Well, that is the Marquis of Mascoso, lover of the widow, the Countess of Villapineda. They say that before he began paying court to her he had sought the hand of a very wealthy man's daughter, but the girl's father, who they say is a trifle close-fisted— but hush! Speaking of the devil—do you see that man closely wrapped in his cloak coming on foot under the arch of San Felipe? Well, he is the father in question. Everybody in Seville knows him on account of his immense fortune.

"Look—look at that group of stately men! They are the twenty-four knights. Aha! there's that Heming, too. They say that the gentlemen of the green cross have not challenged him yet,

99

thanks to his influence with the great ones at
Madrid. All he comes to church for is to hear
the music.

"Alas! neighbor, that looks bad. I fear
there's going to be a scuffle. I shall take refuge
in the church, for, according to my guess, there
will be more blows than *Paternosters*. Look,
look! the Duke of Alcalá's people are coming
round the corner of Saint Peter's Square, and I
think I see the Duke of Medinasidonia's men in
Dueñas Alley. Did n't I tell you? There—
there! The blows are beginning. Neighbor,
neighbor, this way before they close the doors!

"But what 's that? They 've left off. What 's
that light? Torches! a litter! It 's the bishop
himself! God preserve him in his office as many
centuries as I desire to live myself! If it were
not for him, half Seville would have been burned
up by this time with these quarrels of the dukes.
Look at them, look at them, the hypocrites, how
they both press forward to kiss the bishop's ring!

"But come, neighbor—come into the church
before it is packed full. Some nights like this it
is so crowded that you could not get in if you
were no larger than a grain of wheat. The nuns
have a prize in their organist. Other sisterhoods
have made Maese Pérez magnificent offers ; nothing strange about that, though, for the very archbishop has offered him mountains of gold if he
would go to the cathedral. But he would not

listen to them.   He would sooner die than give
up his beloved organ.   You don't know Maese
Pérez?   Oh, I forgot you had just come to the
neighborhood.   Well, he is a holy man; poor, to
be sure, but as charitable as any man that ever
lived.   With no relative but a daughter, and no
friend but his organ, he spends all his time in
caring for the one and repairing the other.   The
organ is an old affair, you must know; but that
makes no difference to him.   He handles it so
that its tone is a wonder.   How he does know it!
and all by touch, too, for did I tell you that the
poor man was born blind?

"Humble, too, as the very stones.   He always
say˘ that he is only a poor convent organist, when
the fact is he could give lessons in *sol fa* to the
very chapel master of the primate.   You see, he
began before he had teeth.   His father had the
same position before him, and as the boy showed
such talent, it was very natural that he should
succeed his father when the latter died.   And
what a touch he has, God bless him!   He always
plays well, always; but on a night like this he is
wonderful.   He has the greatest devotion to this
Christmas Eve mass, and when the host is elevated, precisely at twelve o'clock, which is the
time that Our Lord came into the world, his organ
sounds like the voices of angels.

"But why need I try to tell you about what you
are going to hear to-night?   It is enough for you

to see that all the elegance of Seville, the very archbishop included, comes to a humble convent to listen to him. And it is not only the learned people who can understand his skill that come ; the common people, too, swarm to the church, and are still as the dead when Maese Pérez puts his hand to the organ. And when the host is elevated—when the host is elevated, then you can't hear a fly. Great tears fall from every eye, and when the music is over a long-drawn sigh is heard, showing how the people have been holding their breath all through.

"But come, come, the bells have stopped ringing, and the mass is going to begin. Hurry in. This is Christmas Eve for everybody, but for no one is it a greater occasion than for us."

So saying, the good woman who had been acting as *cicerone* for her neighbor pressed through the portico of the Convent of Santa Inés, and elbowing this one and pushing the other, succeeded in getting inside the church, forcing her way through the multitude that was crowding about the door.

II.

THE church was profusely lighted. The flood of light which fell from the altars glanced from the rich jewels of the great ladies, who, kneeling upon velvet cushions placed before them by pages, and taking their prayer-books from the hands of female attendants, formed a brilliant circle around the chancel lattice. Standing next that lattice, wrapped in their richly colored and embroidered cloaks, letting their green and red orders be seen with studied carelessness, holding in one hand their hats, the plumes sweeping the floor, and letting the other rest upon the polished hilts of rapiers or the jewelled handles of daggers, the twenty-four knights, and a large part of the highest nobility of Seville, seemed to be forming a wall for the purpose of keeping their wives and daughters from contact with the populace. The latter, swaying back and forth at the rear of the nave, with a noise like that of a rising surf, broke out into joyous acclamations as the archbishop was seen to come in. That dignitary seated himself near the high altar under a scarlet canopy, surrounded by his attendants, and three times blessed the people.

It was time for the mass to begin.

Nevertheless, several minutes passed before the celebrant appeared. The multitude commenced to murmur impatiently ; the knights exchanged words with each other in a low tone ; and the archbishop sent one of his attendants to the sacristan to inquire why the ceremony did not begin.

" Maese Pérez has fallen sick, very sick, and

it will be impossible for him to come to the midnight mass."

This was the word brought back by the attendant.

The news ran instantly through the crowd. The disturbance caused by it was so great that the chief judge rose to his feet, and the officers came into the church, to enforce silence.

Just then a man of unpleasant face, thin, bony, and cross-eyed too, pushed up to the place where the archbishop was sitting.

" Maese Pérez is sick," he said ; " the ceremony cannot begin. If you see fit, I will play the organ in his absence. Maese Pérez is not the best organist in the world, nor need this instrument be left unused after his death for lack of any one able to play it."

The archbishop nodded his head in assent, although some of the faithful, who had already recognized in that strange person an envious rival of the organist of Santa Inés, were breaking out in cries of displeasure. Suddenly a surprising noise was heard in the portico.

" Maese Pérez is here !   Maese Pérez is here ! "

At this shout, coming from those jammed in by the door, every one looked around.

Maese Pérez, pale and feeble, was in fact entering the church, brought in a chair which all were quarrelling for the honor of carrying upon their shoulders.

The commands of the physicians, the tears of his daughter—nothing had been able to keep him in bed.

"No," he had said; "this is the last one, I know it. I know it, and I do not want to die without visiting my organ again, this night above all, this Christmas Eve. Come, I desire it, I order it; come, to the church!"

His desire had been gratified. The people carried him in their arms to the organ-loft. The mass began.

Twelve struck on the cathedral clock.

The introit came, then the Gospel, then the offertory, and the moment arrived when the priest, after consecrating the sacred wafer, took it in his hands and began to elevate it. A cloud of incense filled the church in bluish undulations. The little bells rang out in vibrating peals, and Maese Pérez placed his aged fingers upon the organ keys.

The multitudinous voices of the metal tubes gave forth a prolonged and majestic chord, which died away little by little, as if a gentle breeze had borne away its last echoes.

To this opening burst, which seemed like a voice lifted up to heaven from earth, responded a sweet and distant note, which went on swelling and swelling in volume until it became a torrent of overpowering harmony. It was the voice of the angels, traversing space, and reaching the world.

Then distant hymns began to be heard, in-
toned by the hierarchies of seraphim ; a thousand
hymns at once, mingling to form a single one,
though this one was only an accompaniment to a
strange melody which seemed to float above that
ocean of mysterious echoes, as a strip of fog
above the waves of the sea.

One song after another died away.   The movement grew simpler.   Now only two voices were
heard, whose echoes blended.   Then but one
remained, and alone sustained a note as brilliant
as a thread of light.   The priest bowed his face,
and above his gray head appeared the host.   At
that moment the note which Maese Pérez was
holding began to swell and swell, and an explo-
sion of unspeakable joy filled the church.

From each of the notes forming that magnificent chord a theme was developed; and some
near, others far away, these brilliant, those
muffled, one would have said that the waters and
the birds, the breezes and the forests, men and
angels, earth and heaven, were singing, each in
its own language, a hymn in praise of the Saviour's
birth.

The people listened, amazed and breathless.
The officiating priest felt his hands trembling ;
for it seemed as if he had seen the heavens
opened and the host transfigured.

The organ kept on, but its voice sank away
gradually, like a tone going from echo to echo,

and dying as it goes.   Suddenly a cry was heard
in the organ-loft—a piercing, shrill cry, the cry
of a woman.

The organ gave a strange, discordant sound,
like a sob, and then was silent.

The multitude flocked to the stairs leading up
to the organ-loft, towards which the anxious gaze
of the faithful was turned.

"What has happened?   What is the matter?"
one asked the other, and no one knew what to
reply.   The confusion increased.   The excite-
ment threatened to disturb the good order and
decorum fitting within a church.

"What was that?" asked the great ladies of
the chief judge.   He had been one of the first
to ascend to the organ-loft.   Now, pale and displaying signs of deep grief, he was going to the
archbishop, who was anxious, like everybody else,
to know the cause of the disturbance.

"What 's the matter?"

"Maese Pérez has just expired."

In fact, when the first of the faithful rushed
up the stairway, and reached the organ-loft, they
saw the poor organist fallen face down upon the
keys of his old instrument, which was still vibrating, while his daughter, kneeling at his feet, was
vainly calling to him with tears and sobs.

III.

" GOOD-EVENING, my dear Doña Baltasara.
Are you also going to-night to the Christmas
Eve mass? For my part, I was intending to go
to the parish church to hear it, but what has happened—where is Vicente going, do you ask?
Why, where the crowd goes. And I must say,
to tell the truth, that ever since Maese Pérez
died, it seems as if a marble slab was on my heart
whenever I go to Santa Inés. Poor dear man !
He was a saint ! I know one thing—I keep a
piece of his cloak as a relic, and he deserves it.
I solemnly believe that if the archbishop would
stir in the matter, our grandchildren would see
his image among the saints on the altars. But,
of course, he won't do that. The dead and absent have no friends, as they say. It 's all the
latest thing, nowadays ; you understand me.
What? You do not know what has happened?
Well, it 's true you are not exactly in our situation. From our house to the church, and from
the church to our house—a word here and another one there—on the wing—without any
curiosity whatever—I easily find out all the
news.

" Well, then, it 's a settled thing that the organist of San Roman—that squint-eye, who is always slandering other organists—that great blun-
derer, who seems more like a butcher than a

master of *sol fa*—is going to play this Christmas
Eve in Maese Pérez's old place. Of course, you
know, for everybody knows it, and it is a public
matter in all Seville, that no one dared to try
it. His daughter would not, though she is a
professor of music herself. After her father's
death she went into the convent as a novice.
Her unwillingness to play was the most natural
thing in the world ; accustomed as she was to
those marvellous performances, any other playing must have appeared bad to her, not to speak
of her desire to avoid comparisons. But when
the sisterhood had already decided that in honor
of the dead organist, and as a token of respect to
his memory, the organ should not be played to-
night, here comes this fellow along, and says that
he is ready to play it.

" Ignorance is the boldest of all things. It is
true, the fault is not his, so much as theirs who
have consented to this profanation, but that is
the way of the world. But, I say, there 's no
small bit of people coming. Any one would say
that nothing had changed since last year. The
same distinguished persons, the same elegant
costumes, the crowding at the door, the same ex-
citement in the portico, the same throng in the
church. Alas ! if the dead man were to rise, he
would feel like dying again to hear his organ
played by inferior hands. The fact is, if what
the people of the neighborhood tell me is true,

they are getting a fine reception ready for the intruder. When the time comes for him to touch the keys, there is going to break out a racket made by timbrels, drums, and horse-fiddles, so that you can't hear anything else. But hush! there's the hero of the occasion going into the church. Goodness! what gaudy clothes, what a neckcloth, what a high and mighty air! Come, hurry up, the archbishop came only a moment ago, and the mass is going to begin. Come on; I guess this night will give us something to talk about for many a day!"

Saying this, the worthy woman, whom the reader recognizes by her abrupt talkativeness, went into the Church of Santa Inés, opening for herself a path, in her usual way, by shoving and elbowing through the crowd.

The ceremony had already begun. The church was as brilliant as the year before.

The new organist, after passing between the rows of the faithful in the nave, and going to kiss the archbishop's ring, had gone up to the organ-loft, where he was trying one stop of the organ after another, with an affected and ridiculous gravity.

A low, confused noise was heard coming from the common people clustered at the rear of the church, a sure augury of the coming storm, which would not be long in breaking.

" He is a mere clown," said some, " who does

not know how to do anything, not even look straight."

"He is an ignoramus," said others, "who, after having made a perfect rattle out of the organ in his own church, comes here to profane Maese Pérez's."

And while one was taking off his cloak so as to be ready to beat his drum to good advantage, and another was testing his timbrel, and all were more and more buzzing out in talk, only here and there could one be found to defend even feebly that curious person, whose proud and pedantic bearing so strongly contrasted with the modest appearance and kind affability of Maese Pérez.

At last the looked-for moment arrived, when the priest, after bowing low and murmuring the sacred words, took the host in his hands. The bells gave forth a peal, like a rain of crystal notes; the transparent waves of incense rose, and the organ sounded.

But its first chord was drowned by a horrible clamor which filled the whole church. Bagpipes, horns, timbrels, drums, every instrument known to the populace, lifted up their discordant voices all at once.

The confusion and clangor lasted but a few seconds. As the noises began, so they ended, all together.

The second chord, full, bold, magnificent,

sustained itself, pouring from the organ's metal tubes like a cascade of inexhaustible and sonorous harmony.

Celestial songs like those that caress the ear in moments of ecstasy; songs which the soul perceives, but which the lip cannot repeat; single notes of a distant melody, which sound at intervals, borne on the breeze; the rustle of leaves kissing each other on the trees with a murmur like rain; trills of larks which rise with quivering songs from among the flowers like a flight of arrows to the sky; nameless sounds, overwhelming as the roar of a tempest; fluttering hymns, which seemed to be mounting to the throne of the Lord like a mixture of light and sound—all were expressed by the organ's hundred voices, with more vigor, more subtle poetry, more weird coloring, than had ever been known before.

When the organist came down from the loft the crowd which pressed up to the stairway was so great, and their eagerness to see and greet him so intense, that the chief judge, fearing, and not without reason, that he would be suffocated among them all, ordered some of the officers to open a path for the organist, with their staves of office, so that he could reach the high altar, where the prelate was waiting for him.

"You perceive," said the archbishop, " that I have come all the way from my palace to hear

you. Now, are you going to be as cruel as Maese
Pérez ? He would never save me the journey,
by going to play the Christmas Eve mass in the
cathedral."

"Next year," replied the organist, " I promise to give you the pleasure ; since, for all the
gold in the world, I would never play this organ
again."

" But why not ? " interrupted the prelate.

" Because," returned the organist, endeavoring to repress the agitation which revealed itself
in the pallor of his face—" because it is so old
and poor ; one cannot express one's self on it
satisfactorily."

The archbishop withdrew, followed by his attendants. One after another the litters of the
great folk disappeared in the windings of the
neighboring streets. The group in the portico
scattered. The sexton was locking up the doors,
when two women were perceived, who had
stopped to cross themselves and mutter a prayer,
and who were now going on their way into
Dueñas Alley.

"What would you have, my dear Doña Baltasara ? " one was saying. " That's the way I
am. Every crazy person with his whim. The
barefooted Capuchins might assure me that it
was so, and I would not believe it. That man
never played what we have heard. Why, I have
heard him a thousand times in San Bartolomé,
8

his parish church; the priest had to send him
away he was so poor a player. You felt like
plugging your ears with cotton. Why, all you
need is to look at his face, and that is the mirror of the soul, they say. I remember, as if
I was seeing him now, poor man—I remember
Maese Pérez's face, nights like this, when he
came down from the organ-loft, after having en-
tranced the audience with his splendors. What
a gracious smile! What a happy glow on his
face! Old as he was, he seemed like an angel.
But this creature came plunging down as if a dog
were barking at him on the landing, and all
the color of a dead man, while his—come,
dear Doña Baltasara, believe me, and believe
what I say: there is some great mystery about
this."

Thus conversing, the two women turned the
corner of the alley, and disappeared. There is
no need of saying who one of them was.

IV.

ANOTHER year had gone by. The abbess of the
Convent of Santa Inés and Maese Pérez's daughter were talking in a low voice, half hidden in the
shadows of the church choir. The penetrating
voice of the bell was summoning the faithful. A
very few people were passing through the portico,
silent and deserted, this year, and after taking

holy water at the door, were choosing seats in a corner of the nave, where a handful of residents of the neighborhood were quietly waiting for the Christmas Eve mass to begin.

" There, you see," the mother superior was saying, "your fear is entirely childish; there is no one in the church. All Seville is trooping to the cathedral to-night. Play the organ, and do it without any distrust whatever. We are only a sisterhood here. But why don't you speak ? What has happened ? What is the matter with you ?"

" I am afraid," replied the girl, in a tone of the deepest agitation.

" Afraid ! Of what ? "

" I do not know—something supernatural. Listen to what happened last night. I had heard you say that you were anxious for me to play the organ for the mass. I was proud of the honor, and I thought I would arrange the stops and get the organ in good tune so as to give you a surprise to-day. Alone I went into the choir and opened the door leading to the organ-loft. The cathedral clock was striking just then, I do not know what hour ; but the strokes of the bell were very mournful, and they were very numerous— going on sounding for a century, as it seemed to me, while I stood as if nailed to the threshold.

" The church was empty and dark. Far away there gleamed a feeble light, like a faint star in the sky; it was the lamp burning on the high altar. By its flickering light, which only helped to make the deep horror of the shadows the more intense, I saw—I saw—mother, do not disbelieve it—a man. In perfect silence, and with his back turned towards me, he was running over the organ-keys with one hand while managing the stops with the other. And the organ sounded, but in an indescribable manner. It seemed as if each note were a sob smothered in the metal tube, which vibrated under the pressure of the air compressed within it, and gave forth a low, almost imperceptible tone, yet exact and true.

"The cathedral clock kept on striking, and that man kept on running over the keys. I could hear his very breathing.

"Fright had frozen the blood in my veins. My body was as cold as ice, except my head, and that was burning. I tried to cry out, but I could not. That man turned his face and looked at me—no, he did not look at me, for he was blind. It was my father!"

"Nonsense, sister! Banish these fancies with which the adversary endeavors to overturn weak imaginations. Address a *Paternoster* and an *Ave Maria* to the archangel, Saint Michael, the captain of the celestial hosts, that he may aid you in opposing evil spirits. Wear on your neck a scapulary which has been pressed to the relics

of Saint Pacomio, the counsellor against tempta-
tions, and go, go quickly, and sit at the organ.
The mass is going to begin, and the faithful are
growing impatient. Your father is in heaven,
and thence, instead of giving you a fright, will
descend to inspire his daughter in the solemn
service."

The prioress went to occupy her seat in the
choir in the midst of the sisterhood. Maese
Pérez's daughter opened the door of the organ-
loft with trembling hand, sat down at the organ,
and the mass began.

The mass began, and went on without anything
unusual happening until the time of consecration
came. Then the organ sounded. At the same
time came a scream from Maese Pérez's daughter.

The mother superior, the nuns, and some of
the faithful rushed up to the organ-loft.

"Look at him!—look at him!" cried the girl,
fixing her eyes, starting from their sockets, upon
the seat, from which she had risen in terror. She
was clinging with convulsed hands to the railing
of the organ-loft.

Everybody looked intently at the spot to which
she directed her gaze. No one was at the organ,
yet it went on sounding—sounding like the
songs of the archangels in their bursts of mystic
ecstasy.

"Did n't I tell you a thousand times, if I did

once, dear Doña Baltasara—did n't I tell you? There is some great mystery about this. What! did n't you go last night to the Christmas Eve mass? Well, you must know, anyhow, what happened. Nothing else is talked about in the whole city. The archbishop is furious, and no wonder. Not to have gone to Santa Inés, not to have been present at the miracle—and all to hear a wretched clatter! That 's all the inspired organist of San Bartolomé made in the cathedral, so persons who heard him tell me. Yes, I said so all the time. The squint-eye never could have played that. It was all a lie. There is some great mystery here. What do I think it was? Why, it was the soul of Maese Pérez."

MOORS AND CHRISTIANS
BY
PÉDRO ANTONIO DE ALARCÓN

From " Moors and Christians," by Pédro Antonio de
Alarcon.   Translated by Mary J. Serrano.

MOORS AND CHRISTIANS

BY PEDRO ANTONIO DE ALARCÓN

I.

THE once famous but now little known town of Aldeire is situated in the Marquisate of El Cenét, or, let us say, on the eastern slope of the Alpujarra, and partly hangs over a ledge, partly hides itself in a ravine of the giant central ridge of Sierra Nevada, five or six thousand feet above the level of the sea, and seven or eight thousand below the eternal snows of the Aulhacem.

Aldeire, be it said with all respect to its reverend pastor, is a Moorish town. That it was formerly Moorish is clearly proved by its name, its situation, and its architecture, and that it is not yet completely Christianized, although it figures among the towns of reconquered Spain, and has its little Catholic church and its confraternities of the Virgin, of Jesus, and of several of the saints, is proved by the character and the customs of its inhabitants ; by the perpetual feuds, as terrible as they are causeless, which

unite or separate them ; and by the gloomy black
eyes, pale complexions, laconic speech, and in-
frequent laughter of men, women, and children.

But it may be well to remind our readers, in
order that neither the aforesaid pastor nor any
one else may question the justice of this reasoning, that the Moors of the Marquisate of El
Cenét were not expelled in a body, like those of
the Alpujarra, but that many of them succeeded
in remaining in the country, living in concealment, thanks to the prudence—or the cowardice
—which made them turn a deaf ear to the rash
and the heroic appeal of their unfortunate Prince,
Aben Humcya; whence I infer that Uncle Juan
Gomez, nicknamed Hormiga,* in the year of
grace 1821 Constitutional Alcalde of Aldeire,
might very well be the descendant of some Mus-
tapha, Mohammed, or the like.

It is related, then, that the aforesaid Juan
Gomez—a man at the time of our story about
fifty years of age, very shrewd, although he knew
neither how to read nor write, and grasping and
industrious to some purpose, as might be inferred
not only from his *sobriquet*, but also from his
wealth, acquired honestly or otherwise, and in-
vested in the most fertile lands of the district—
leased, at a nominal rent, by means of a present
to the secretary of the corporation of some hens
which had left off laying, a piece of arid town

* The Ant.

land, on which stood an old ruin, formerly a Moorish watch-tower or hermitage, and still called the Moor's Tower.

Needless to say that Uncle Hormiga did not stop to consider for an instant who this Moor might be, nor what might have been the original purpose of the ruined building ; the one thing which he saw at once, clear as water, was, that with the stones which had already fallen from the ruin and those which he should remove from it, he might make a secure and commodious yard for his cattle ; consequently, on the very day after it came into his possession, and as a suitable pastime for a man of his thrifty habits, he began to devote his leisure hours to the task of pulling down what still remained standing of the ruin.

" You will kill yourself," said his wife, seeing him come home in the evening, covered with dust and sweat and carrying his crowbar hidden under his cloak.

"On the contrary," he answered, " this exercise is good for me ; it will put my blood in motion and keep me from being like our sons, the students who, according to what the storekeeper tells me, were at the theatre in Granada the other night looking so yellow that it was enough to make one sick to see them."

" Poor boys ! From studying so much ! But you ought to be ashamed to work like a laborer, when you are the richest man in the town, and Alcalde into the bargain."

"That is why I take no one with me. Here, hand me that salad ! "

" It would be well to have some one to help you, however. You will spend an age in pulling down the tower by yourself, and besides, you may not be able to manage it."

"Don't talk nonsense, Torcuata. When I begin to build the wall of the cattle yard, I shall hire workmen, and even employ a master-builder. But any one can pull down. And it is such fun to destroy ! Come, clear away the table and let us go to bed."

" You speak that way because you are a man. As for me, it disturbs and saddens me to see things destroyed."

" Old women's notions. If you only knew how many things there are in the world that ought to be destroyed ! "

" Hold your tongue, you free-mason ! It was a misfortune they ever elected you Alcalde. You will see when the Royalists come into power again that the king will have you hanged ! "

"Yes, we shall see ! Bigot ! Hypocrite ! Owl ! Come, I am sleepy ; stop blessing your-self and put out that light. "

And thus they would argue until one or the other of the consorts fell asleep.

II.

ONE evening Uncle Hormiga returned from his task very thoughtful and preoccupied, and earlier than usual.

His wife waited until after he had dismissed the laborers to ask him what was the matter, when he responded by showing her a leaden tube with a cover, somewhat like the tube in which a soldier on furlough keeps his leave, from which he drew a yellow parchment covered with crabbed handwriting, and carefully unrolling it said, with imposing gravity :

" I don't know how to read, even in Spanish, which is the easiest language in the world, but the devil take me if this was not written by a Moor."

" That is to say that you found it in the tower ? "

" I don't say it on that account alone, but because these spider's legs don't look like anything I ever saw written by a Christian."

The wife of Juan Gomez looked at the parch-ment, smelled it, and exclaimed, with a confi-dence as amusing as it was ill-founded :

" By a Moor it was written ! "

After a while she added, with a melancholy air :

" Although I am but a poor hand myself at reading writing, I would swear that we hold in our hands the discharge of some soldier of Mohammed who is now in the bottomless pit."

" You say that on account of the tube."

"On account of the tube I say it."

"Well, then, you are altogether wrong, my dear Torcuata, for such a thing as conscription was not known among the Moors, nor is this a discharge. This is a—a—"

Uncle Hormiga glanced around him cautiously, lowered his voice, and said with air of absolute certainty :

"This paper contains directions where to find a treasure ! "

" You are right ! " cried his wife, suddenly inspired with the same belief ; "and have you already found it ? Is it very big ? Did you cover it up carefully again ? Are the coins gold or silver ? Do you think they will pass current now ? What a happiness for our boys ! How they will spend money and enjoy themselves in Granada and Madrid ! I want to have a look at it. Let us go there. There is a moon to-night ! "

" Silly woman ! Be quiet ! How do you suppose that I could find the treasure by these directions, when I don't know how to read, either in Moorish or in Christian ? "

" That's true ! Well, then, I 'll tell you what to do. As soon as it is daylight, saddle a good mule, cross the Sierra through the Puerto de la

Ragua, which they say is safe now, and go to Ugíjar, to the house of our gossip, Don Matías Quesada, who knows something of everything. He will explain what is in the paper and give you good advice, as he always does."

"And money enough his advice has cost me, notwithstanding our gossipred! But I was thinking of doing that myself. In the morning I will start for Ugíjar and be back by nightfall ; I can do that easily by putting the mule to his speed."

"But be sure and explain everything to him clearly."

"I have very little to explain. The tube was hidden in a hollow, or niche, in the wall, and covered with tiles, like those at Valencia. I tore down the whole of the wall, but I found nothing else. At the surface of the ground begin the foundation walls, built of immense stones, more than a yard square, any one of which it would take two or three men as strong as I am to move. Consequently, it is necessary to know exactly where the treasure is hidden, unless we want to tear up all the foundation walls of the tower, which could not be done without outside help."

"No, no; set out for Ugíjar as soon as it is daybreak Offer our gossip a part—not a large one—of what we may find, and as soon as we know where we must dig, I will help you myself to tear up the foundation stones. My darling boys! It is all for them! For my part, the only thing that troubles me is lest there be some sin in this business that we are whispering about."

"What sin can there be in it, you great fool?"

"I can't explain what I mean, but treasures have always seemed to me to have something to do with the devil, or the fairies. And then, you got that ground for so low a rent! The whole town says there was some trickery in the business!"

"That concerns the secretary and councillors. They drew up the documents."

"Besides, as I understand, when a treasure is discovered, a part of it must be given to the king."

"That is when it is found on ground that is not one's own, like mine!"

"One's own! One's own! Who knows to whom that tower the Council sold you belonged!"

"Why, to the Moor, of course!"

"And who knows who that Moor may have been? It seems to me, Juan, whatever money the Moor may have hidden in his house should belong to him, or to his heirs, not to you or to me."

"You are talking nonsense. According to that, it is not I who ought to be the Alcalde of Aldeire, but the man who was Alcalde a year ago, at the time of the proclamation of Riego. According to that, we should have to send the rents of the lands of Granada and Guadix, and hundreds of other towns, every year to the descendants of the Moors in Africa."

"It may be that you are right. At any rate, go to Ugíjar, and our gossip will tell you what is best to be done in the matter."

III.

Ugíjar is distant from Aldeire some four leagues, and the road between the two towns is a very bad one. Before nine o'clock on the following morning, however, Uncle Juan Gomez, wearing his blue stockinet knee-breeches and his embroidered white Sunday boots, was in the office of Don Matías de Quesada, a vigorous old man, a doctor in civil and criminal jurisprudence, and the most noted criminal lawyer in that part of the country. He had always been a promoter of lawsuits, and was very wealthy, and had a large circle of influential acquaintances in Granada and Madrid.

When he had heard his worthy gossip's story and had carefully examined the paper, he gave it as his opinon that the document had nothing whatever to do with the treasure; that the hole in which the tube had been found was a sort of closet, and the writing one of the prayers which

9

the Moors read every Friday morning. But not-withstanding this, as he was not thoroughly versed in the Arabic language, he added that he would send the document to a college companion of his who was employed in the Commission of the Holy Places, in Madrid, in order that he might send it to Jerusalem, where it could be translated into Spanish, for which purpose it would be well to inclose to his friend in Madrid a draft for a couple of ounces in gold, for a cup of chocolate.

Uncle Juan Gomez considered seriously before he made up his mind to pay so high a price for a cup of chocolate (which would be paying for the article at the rate of 10,240 reals a pound), but he was so certain in regard to the treasure (and in truth he was not mistaken, as we shall see later on), that he took from his belt eight gold pieces of four dollars each and delivered them to Don Matías, who weighed them one by one before putting them into his purse, after which Hormiga took the road back to Aldeire, resolving in his own mind to continue his excavations under the Moor's tower while the document went to the Holy Land and came back translated ; proceed-ings which, according to the lawyer, would oc-cupy something like a year and a half.

IV.

UNCLE JUAN had no sooner turned his back upon his gossip and counsellor than the latter took his pen and wrote the following letter :

"*Don Bonifacio Tudela y Gonzalez, Chapel-master of the Cathedral of Ceuta.*

"MY DEAR NEPHEW-IN-LAW,—To no one but a man of your piety would I confide the important secret contained in the accompanying document. I say important, because without a doubt in it are directions for finding the hiding-place of a *treasure*, of which I will give you a part if I should succeed in discovering it with your help. To this end you must get a Moor to translate the document for you and send me the translation in a certified letter, mentioning the matter to no one, unless it be your wife, whom I know to be a person of discretion.

"Forgive my not having written to you in all these years, but you know how busy a life I lead. Your aunt continues to remember you in her prayers every night. I hope you are better of the affection of the stomach from which you were suffering in 1806, and remain your affectionate uncle-in-law,

"MATÍAS DE QUESADA.

"UGÍJAR, *January* 15, 1821.

"P. S.—Regards to Pepa, and tell me when you write if you have any children."

Having written this letter, the distinguished jurisconsult bent his steps toward the kitchen, where his wife was engaged in knitting and minding the *olla*, and throwing into her lap the four golden coins he had received from Juan Gomez, he said to her, in a harsh, cross voice :

" There, Encarnacion, buy more wheat; it is going to rise in price during the dear months; and see to it that you get good measure. Get my breakfast ready while I go post this letter for Seville, inquiring the price of barley. Let the egg be well done and don't let the chocolate be muddy, as it usually is."

The lawyer's wife answered not a word, but went on with her knitting, like an automaton.

V.

Two weeks later, on a beautiful day in January, a day such as is to be seen only in the north of Africa and the south of Europe, the Chapel-master of the cathedral of Ceuta was enjoying the sunshine on the roof of his two-story house, with the tranquillity of mind proper to one who had played the organ at high mass and had afterward eaten a pound of anchovies, another of meat, and another of bread, and drank the corresponding quantity of Tarifa wine.

The worthy musician, who was as fat as a hog

and as red as a beet, was slowly digesting his breakfast, while his lethargic gaze slowly wandered over the magnificent panorama of the Mediterranean,—the Straits of Gibraltar, the accursed rock from which they take their name, the neighboring peaks of Anghera and Benzú, and the distant snows of the Lesser Atlas—when he heard hasty steps on the stairs and his wife's silvery voice crying joyfully:

"Bonifacio! Bonifacio! A letter from your uncle! And a heavy letter, too!"

"Well," answered the Chapel-master, turning around like a geographical sphere or globe on the point on which his rotund personality rested on the seat, "what saint can have put it into my uncle's head to remember me? I have been living for fifteen years in this country usurped from Mohammed, and this is the first time that Abencerrage has written to me, although I have written to him a hundred times. Doubtless he wants me to render him some service."

So saying, he opened the epistle, contriving so that the Pepa of the postscript should not be able to read its contents, and the yellow parchment, noisily unfolding itself, greeted their eyes.

"What has he sent us?" asked his wife, a native of Cadiz, and a blonde, attractive and fresh-looking, notwithstanding her forty summers.

"Don't be inquisitive, Pepita. I will tell you what is in the letter, if I think you ought to know, as soon as I have read it. I have warned you a thousand times to respect my letters."

"A proper precaution for a libertine like you! At any rate be quick, and let us see if I may know what that large paper is that your uncle has sent you. It looks like a bank-note from the other world."

While his wife was making these and other observations, the musician finished reading the letter, whose contents surprised him so greatly that he rose to his feet without the slightest effort.

Dissimulation was so habitual with him, however, that he was able to say, in a natural tone of voice :

"What nonsense! The wretched man is no doubt already in his dotage! Would you believe that he sends me this leaf from a Hebrew Bible, in order that I may look for some Jew who will buy it, the foolish creature supposing that he will get a fortune for it. At the same time," he added, to change the conversation, putting the letter and the parchment into his pocket,—"at the same time, he asks me with much interest if we have any children."

"He has none himself," cried Pepita quickly. "No doubt he intends to leave us something."

"It is more likely the miserly fellow thinks of our leaving him something. But hark, it is striking eleven. It is time for me to go tune the organ

for vespers. I must go now. Listen, my treasure ; let dinner be ready by one, and don't forget
to put a couple of good potatoes into the pot.
Have we any children ! I am ashamed to tell
him we have none. See, Pepa," said the musician, after a moment, having in mind, no doubt,
the Arabic document, " if my uncle should
make me his heir, or if I should ever grow rich
by any other means, I swear that I will take you
to the Plaza of San Antonio in Cadiz to live, and
I will buy you more jewels than Our Lady of Sor-
rows of Granada has. So good-bye for a while,
my pigeon."

And, pinching his wife's dimpled chin, he took
his hat and turned his steps—not in the direction
of the cathedral, but in that of the poor quarter
of the town in which the Moorish citizens of
Ceuta for the most part live.

VI.

In one of the narrowest streets of this quarter,
seated on the floor or rather on his heels, at the
door of a very modest but very neat whitewashed
house, smoking a clay pipe, was a Moor of some
thirty-five or forty years of age, a dealer in eggs
and chickens, which the free peasants of Sierra
Bullones and Sierra Bermeja brought to him to
the gates of Ceuta, and which he sold either in
his own house or at the market, with a profit of

a hundred per cent.   He wore a white woollen *chivala* and a black woollen, hooded Arab cloak, and was called by the Spaniards, Manos-gordas, and by the Moors, Admet-Ben-Carime-el-Abdoun.

When the Moor saw the Chapel-master approaching, he rose and advanced to meet him, making deep salaams at every step, and when they were close together, he said cautiously :

" You want a little Moorish girl ?   I bring to-morrow little dark girl of twelve—"

" My wife wants no more Moorish servants," answered the musician stiffly.

Manos-gordas began to laugh.

" Besides," continued Don Bonifacio, " your infernal little Moorish girls are very dirty."

" Wash ! " responded the Moor, extending his arms crosswise and inclining his head to one side.

" I tell you I want no Moorish girls," said Don Bonifacio.   " What I want to-day is that you, who know so much that you are Interpreter of the Fortress, should translate this document into Spanish for me."

Manos-gordas took the document, and at the first glance murmured :

" It is Moor—"

" Of course, it is in Arabic.   But I want to know what it says, and if you do not deceive me I will give you a handsome present—when the business which I am about to entrust you with is concluded."

Meantime Admet-Ben-Carime glanced his eye over the document, turning very pale as he did so.

"You see that it concerns a great treasure?" the Chapel-master half-affirmed, half-asked.

"Me think so," stammered the Mohammedan.

"What do you mean by saying you think so? Your very confusion tells plainly that it is so."

"Pardon," replied Manos-gordas, a cold sweat breaking out over his body. "Here words modern Arabic—I understand. Here words ancient, or classic Arabic—I no understand."

"What do the words that you understand signify?"

"They signify *gold*, they signify *pearls*, they signify *curse of Alà*. But I no understand meaning, explanations, or signs. Must see the Dervish of Anghera—wise man and translate all. I take parchment to-day and bring parchment to-morrow, and deceive not nor rob Señor Tudela. Moor swear."

Saying which he clasped his hands together, and, raising them to his lips, kissed them fervently.

Don Bonifacio reflected ; he knew that in order to decipher the meaning of this document he should be obliged to take some Moor into his confidence, and there was none with whom he was so well acquainted and who was so well disposed to him as Manos-gordas ; he consented, therefore, to confide the manuscript to him, making him swear repeatedly that he would return on the following day from Anghera with the translation, and swearing to the Moor on his side that he would give him at least a hundred dollars when the treasure should be discovered.

The Mussulman and the Christian then separated, and the latter directed his steps, not to his own house, nor to the cathedral, but to the office of a friend of his, where he wrote the following letter :

" *Senor Don Matías de Quesada y Sanchez, Alpujarra, Ugíjar.*

" MY DEAREST UNCLE,—Thanks be to God that we have at last received news of you and of Aunt Encarnacion, and as good news as Josefa and I could desire. We, my dear uncle, although younger than you and my aunt, are full of ailments and burdened with children, who will soon be left orphans and compelled to beg for their bread.

" Whoever told you that the document you sent me bore any reference to a treasure deceived you. I have had it translated by a competent person, and it turns out to be a string of blasphemies against our Lord Jesus Christ, the Holy Virgin, and the Saints, written in Arabic verses, by a Moorish dog of the Marquisate of El Cenét, during the rebellion of Aben-Humeya. In view of its sacrilegious nature, and by the advice of the Señor Penitentiary, I have just burned this impious testimony to Mohammedan perversity.

"Remembrances to my aunt ; Josefa desires to be remembered to you both ; she is now for the tenth time in an interesting condition, and your nephew, who is reduced to skin and bone by the wretched affection of the stomach, which you will remember, begs that you will send him some assistance.

"BONIFACIO.

"CEUTA, *January* 29, 1821."

VII.

WHILE the Chapel-master was writing and posting this letter, Admet-el-Abdoun was gathering together in a bundle all his wearing apparel and household belongings, consisting of three old hooded mantles, two cloaks of goat's wool, a mortar for grinding alcazuz, an iron lamp, and a copper skillet full of *pesetas*, which he dug up from a corner of the little yard of his house. He loaded with all this his one wife, slave, odalisque, or whatever she might be, a woman uglier than an unexpected piece of bad news, and filthier than her husband's conscience, and issued forth from Ceuta, telling the soldier on guard at the gate opening on the Moorish country that they were going to Fez for change of air, by the advice of a veterinary; and as from that day—now more than sixty years ago—to this no one in Ceuta or its neighborhood has ever again seen Manos-gordas, it is obvious that Don Bonifacio Tudela y Gonzalez had not the satisfaction of receiving from his hands the translation of the document, either on the following, or on any other day during the remainder of his existence; which, indeed, cannot have been very long, since, according to reliable information, it appears that his adored Pepita took to herself, after his death, anotner husband, an Asturian drum-major residing in Marbella, whom she presented with four children, beautiful as the sun, and that she was again a widow at the time of the death of the king, at which epoch she gained, by competition in Malaga, the title of gossip and the position of matron in the custom-house.

And now let us follow Manos-gordas and learn what became of him and of the mysterious document.

VIII.

ADMET-BEN-CARIME-EL-ABDOUN breathed freely, and even danced a few steps for joy, without dancing off his ill-fastened slippers, however, as soon as he found himself outside the massive walls of the Spanish fortress and with all Africa before him.

For Africa, for a true African like Manos-gordas, is the land of absolute liberty; of a liberty anterior and superior to all human con-stitutions and institutions; of a liberty resem-bling that enjoyed by the wild rabbits and other wild animals of the mountain, the valley, or the desert.

By this I mean to say that Africa is the para-dise of evil-doers, the safe asylum, the neutral ground of both men and beasts, protected here by the intense heat and the vast extent of the des-erts. As for the sultans, kings, and beys who fancy they rule here, and the authorities and sol-diers who represent them, it may be said that they are for such subjects what the hunter is for the hare or for the stag—a misadventure which one in a hundred may chance to meet with, and which may or may not result fatally; if he who meets it dies, he is remembered on the anniversary of his death; and if he does not die, he takes himself off to a sufficient distance from the scene of his mishap—and no more is thought about the mat-ter. With this digression we will now resume the thread of our story.

"This way, Zama!" cried the Moor to his weary consort, as if he were calling to a beast of burden.

And instead of turning eastward, that is to say toward the gap of Anghera, in quest of the holy sage, in accordance with his promise to Don

Bonifacio, he proceeded southward along a ravine overgrown with wild brambles and forest trees which soon brought him to the Tetuán road ; that is to say, to the indistinct footpath which, following the indentations of the coast, leads to Cape Negro by the valley of the Tarajar, the valley of the Castillejos, Mount Negro, and the lakes of Azmir River, names which are now heard by every true Spaniard with love and veneration, but which at the time of our story had not yet been pronounced either in Spain or in any other part of the civilized world.

When Ben-Carime and Zama had reached the little valley of the Tarajar, they sat down to rest for a while at the edge of the rivulet which, rising in the heights of Sierra Bullones, runs through it, and in this wild and secluded spot, that seemed as if it had come fresh from the Creator's hand and had never yet been trod by the foot of man, looking out on the solitary ocean, whose waters were untracked save, on an occasional moonlight night, by some pirate caravel or government vessel sent from Europe in pursuit of it, the Moorish woman proceeded to make her toilet, performing her ablutions in the stream, and the Moor unfolded the manuscript and read it again, manifesting no less emotion than he had shown on the previous occasion.

The contents of the Arabian manuscript were as follows :

" May the benediction of Allah rest on all good men who read these lines !

" There is no glory but the glory of Allah, whose prophet and messenger Mohammed was and is, in the hearts of the faithful.

" May those who rob the house of him who is at the wars, or in exile, be accursed of Allah and of Mohammed, and die eaten up by beetles and cockroaches !

" Blessed be Allah, who created these and other vermin to devour the wicked !

" I am the *caid* Hassan-ben-Jussef, the servant of Allah, although I am miscalled Don Rodrigo de Acuña by the successors of the Christian dogs who, by force and in violation of solemn compact, baptized, with a broom of hyssop, my ill-fated ancestors, together with many other Islamites of these kingdoms.

" I am a captain, serving under the banner of him whose lawful title, since the death of Aben-Humaya, is King of Andalusia, Muley-Abdallah-Mahamud-Aben-Aboó, who does not now sit on the throne of Granada because of the treachery and cowardice with which the Moors of Valencia broke their oaths and compacts, failing to rise with the Moors of Granada against the common enemy; but they will receive their reward from Allah, and if we are conquered, they, too, will be conquered and in the end expelled from Spain, without the merit of having fought to the last on the field of honor in defence of their rights ; and if we are the conquerors we will cut off their heads and throw them to the swine.

"I am, in conclusion, the lord of this tower and of all the land surrounding it, westward to the ravine of the Fox and eastward to the ravine of the Asparagus, so called from the luxuriant growth and exquisite flavor of the asparagus cultivated there by my grandfather, Sidi-Jussef-ben-Jussuf.

"Things are going badly with us. Since the coming of the base-born Don Juan of Austria (whom may Allah confound !) to fight against the faithful, we have foreseen that, for the present, we shall be defeated, although in the course of years or of centuries another Prince of the blood of the Prophet may recover the throne of Granada which for seven hundred years was in the possession of the Moors, and which will be theirs again when Allah wills it, by the same right by which it was formerly possessed by the Goths and Vandals, and before that by the Romans, and before that by those other Africans, the Carthaginians—by the right of conquest. But I know, as I have said, that, for the present, things are going badly with us, and that I must very soon depart for Morocco, taking with me my forty-three sons; that is to say, unless the Austrians capture me in the coming battle and hang me on a tree, as I would hang all of them, if it were in my power to do so.

"Well, then, when I depart from this tower to engage in the last and the decisive campaign, I leave hidden here, in a place which no one can discover without coming across this manuscript, all my gold, all my silver, all my pearls, my family treasures, the possessions of my fathers, of myself, and of my heirs; the fortune of which I am lord and master by human and divine right, as the bird is of its feathers, or the child of the teeth he cuts with suffering, or as every mortal is of the bad humors, cancerous or leprous, which he may inherit from his ancestors.

"Stay thy hand, then, oh thou, Moor, Christian, or Jew, who, in tearing down this, my dwelling, mayest discover and read these lines which I am now writing! Stay thy hand and respect the treasure-house of thy fellow-mortal! Touch not his estate! Take not possession of that which belongs to another! Here there is none of the public wealth, nothing belonging to the exchequer, nothing belonging to the state. The gold in the mine may belong of right to him who discovers it, and a part of it to the king of the country; but gold melted down and stamped—money, coin—belongs to its owner and to no one but its owner. Rob me not, therefore, evil man! Rob not my descendants who will come, on the day appointed, to take possession of their inheritance. And if thou shouldst, without evil intent, and by chance discover my

10

treasure, I counsel thee to make public proclamation, calling on and notifying the circum-
stance to the heirs of Hassan-ben-Jussef; for it
is not just to keep that which has been found
when it has a lawful owner.

"If thou doest not this, be accursed, with the
curse of Allah, and with my curse! And mayest
thou be struck dead by lightning! And may each
coin of my money and each pearl of my treasure
become a scorpion in thy hands! And may thy
children die of leprosy, may their fingers rot and
drop off, so that they may not have even the
pleasure of scratching themselves! And may
the woman thou lovest love thy slave and betray
thee for him. And may thy eldest daughter leave
thy house secretly with a Jew! And mayest thou
be impaled upon a stake, and suspended on high,
exposed to the public gaze, until by the weight of
thy body the stake pierce thy crown and thou fall
parted asunder on the ground like a loathsome
toad cut in twain by the hoe!

"Now thou knowest what I would have thee
know, and let all men know it, and blessed be
Allah who is Allah!

"Tower of Zoraya, in Aldeire, in El Cenét,
On the fifteenth day of the month of Saphar,
Of the year of the Hegira 968.

"HASSEN-BEN-JUSSEF."

IX.

MANOS-GORDAS was profoundly impressed by a second reading of this document ; not because of the moral maxims or the terrible curses it contained, for the rascal had lost his faith both in Allah and in Mohammed, through his frequent intercourse with the Christians and the Jews of Tetuan and Ceuta, who naturally scoffed at the Koran, but because he believed that his face, his accent, and some other personal peculiarities of his forbade his going to Spain, where he would find himself exposed to certain death should any Christian man or woman discover him to be an enemy to the Virgin Mary.

" Besides, what aid " (in the opinion of Manos-gordas) " could a foreigner, a Mohammedan, a semi-barbarian, expect from the laws or the authorities of Spain, in acquiring possession of the Tower of Zoraya for the purpose of making excavations there, or what protection in retaining possession of the treasure when he should have discovered it, or even of his life ? There is no help for it," was the conclusion to which he came, after much reflection. " I must trust the secret to the renegade Ben-Munuza. He is a Spaniard, and his companionship will protect me from danger in that country. But as there does not exist under the canopy of heaven a wickeder

man than this same renegade, it will not be amiss
to take some precautions."

And, as a result of his reflections, he took
from his pocket writing materials, wrote a letter,
and inclosed it in an envelope, which he sealed
with a bit of moistened bread, and this done, he
burst into a sardonic laugh.

He then looked at his wife, who was still engaged in removing the filth of an entire year from
her person, at the expense of the material and
moral cleanliness of the poor rivulet, and having
attracted her attention by a whistle, he deigned
to address her in these terms:

"Sit down here beside me, fig-face, and listen
to what I am going to say. You can afterward
finish washing yourself—and well you need it—
and perhaps I may then think you worthy of
something better than the daily drubbing by
which I show my affection for you. But for the
present, brazenface, leave off your grimaces, and
listen well to what I am going to tell you."

The Moorish woman, who after her toilet
looked younger and more artistic, though no less
ugly than before, licked her lips like a cat, fixed
the two carbuncles that served her for eyes on
Manos-gordas, and said, showing her broad white
teeth, that bore no resemblance to those of a
human being:

"Speak, my lord, your slave desires only to
serve you."

Manos-gordas continued :

" If, in the future, any misfortune should happen to me, or if I should suddenly disappear without taking leave of you, or if, after taking leave of you, you should hear nothing from me within six weeks' time, make your way back to Ceuta and put this letter in the post. Do you understand fully what I have said, monkey-face ? "

Zama burst into tears and exclaimed :

" Admet, do you intend to abandon me ? "

" Don't be an ass, woman ! " answered the Moor. " Who is talking of such a thing now? You know very well that you please me and that you are useful to me. The question now is whether you have understood my charge perfectly."

" Give it here ! " said the Moorish woman, taking the letter and placing it in her dark-skinned bosom, next her heart. " If any evil should happen to you, this letter shall be placed in the post at Ceuta, though I should drop dead the moment after."

Aben-Carime smiled with a human smile when he heard these words, and deigned to let his eyes rest upon his wife as if she were a human being.

X.

The Moorish couple must have slept soundly and sweetly among the thickets on the roadside that night, for it was fully nine o'clock on the following morning when they reached the foot of Cape Negro.

At that place there is a village of Arab shepherds and husbandmen, called Medick, consisting of a few huts, a *morabito* or Mohammedan hermitage, and a well of fresh water, with its curbstone and its copper bucket, like the wells we see represented in certain biblical scenes.

At this hour the village was completely deserted, its inhabitants having betaken themselves, with their cattle and their implements of labor, to the neighboring hills and glens.

" Wait for me here," said Manos-gordas to his wife. " I am going in quest of Ben-Munuza, who at this hour is probably ploughing his fields on the other side of yonder hill."

" Ben-Munuza ! " exclaimed Zama, with a look of terror ; " the renegade of whom you spoke to me ? "

" Make your mind easy," returned Manos-gordas. " I have the upper hand now. In a few hours I shall be back and you will see him following me like a dog. This is his cabin. Wait for us inside, and make us a good mess of alcazus, with the maize and the butter you will find at hand. You know I like it well cooked. Ah, I forgot. If I should not be back before nightfall, ascend the hill, cross over to the other side, and if you do not find me there, or if you should find my dead body, return to Ceuta and post this letter.—Another thing: if you should find me dead, search my clothing for this parchment; if you do not find it upon me, you will know that Ben-Munuza has robbed me of it; in which case proceed from Ceuta to Tetuan and denounce him as a thief and an assassin to the authorities. That is all I have to tell you. Farewell!"

The Moorish woman wept bitterly as Manosgordas took the path that led to the summit of the neighboring hill.

XI.

On reaching the other side of the hill Manosgordas descried in a glen, a short distance off, a corpulent Moor dressed in white, ploughing the black earth with the help of a fine yoke of oxen, in patriarchal fashion. This man, who seemed a statue of Peace carved in marble, was the morose and dreaded renegade, Ben-Munuza, the details of whose story would make the reader shudder with horror, if he were to hear them.

Suffice it for the present to say that he was some forty years old, that he was active, vigorous, and robust, and that he was of a gloomy cast

of countenance, although his eyes were blue as
the sky, and his beard yellow as the African sun-
light, which had bronzed his originally fair complexion.

"Good-morning, Manos-gordas!" cried the
renegade, as soon as he perceived the Moor.

And his voice expressed the melancholy pleasure the exile feels in a foreign land when he
meets some one with whom he can converse in
his native tongue.

"Good-morning, Juan Falgueira!" responded
Ben-Carime, in ironical accents.

As he heard this name the renegade trembled
from head to foot, and seizing the iron bar of
the plough prepared to defend himself.

"What name is that you have just pronounced?" he said, advancing threateningly toward Manos-gordas.

The latter awaited his approach, laughing, and
answered in Arabic, with a courage which no
one would have supposed him to possess :

"I have pronounced your real name ; the
name you bore in Spain when you were a Christian, and which I learned when I was in Orán
three years ago."

"In Orán?"

"Yes, in Orán. What is there extraordinary
in that? You had come from Orán to Morocco ;
I went to Orán to buy hens. I inquired there
concerning your history, describing your appear-

ance, and some Spaniards living there related it
to me. I learned that you were a Galician, that
your name was Juan Falgueira, and that you had
escaped from the prison of Granada, on the eve
of the day appointed for your execution, for having robbed and murdered, fifteen years ago, a
party of gentlemen, whom you were serving in
the capacity of muleteer. Do you still doubt
that I know who you are ? "

" Tell me, my soul," responded the renegade,
in a hollow voice, looking cautiously around,
" have you related this story to any of the Moors ?
Does any one but yourself in this accursed land
know it ? Because the fact is, I want to live in
peace, without having any one or anything to
remind me of that fatal deed which I have well
expiated. I am a poor man. I have neither
family, nor country, nor language, nor even the
God who made me left to me. I live among
enemies, with no other wealth than these oxen
and these fields, bought by the fruit of ten years'
sweat and toil. Consequently, you do very wrong
to come and tell me—"

" Hold ! " cried Manos-gordas, greatly alarmed.
" Don't cast those wolfish glances at me, for I
come to do you a great service, and not to vex
you needlessly. I have told your unfortunate
story to no one. What for ? Any secret may be
a treasure, which he who tells gives away. There
are, however, occasions in which an *exchange of*

secrets may be made with profit. For instance, I am going to tell you an important secret of mine, which will serve as security for yours, and which will oblige us to be friends for the rest of our lives."

" I am listening; go on," responded the renegade quietly.

Aben-Carime then read aloud the Arabic document, which Juan Falgueira listened to without moving a muscle of his still angry countenance. The Moor seeing this, in order to dispel his distrust, disclosed to him the fact that he had stolen the paper he had just read from a Christian in Ceuta.

The Spaniard smiled slightly to think how great must be the huckster's fear of him to cause him voluntarily to reveal to him his theft, and poor Manos-gordas, encouraged by Ben-Munuza's smile, proceeded to disclose his plans, in the following terms :

" I take it for granted that you understand perfectly well the importance of this document and the reason of my reading it to you. I know not where the Tower of Zoraya, nor Aldeire, nor El Cenét is, nor do I know how to go to Spain, nor should I be able to find my way through that country if I were there ; besides which, the people would kill me for not being a Christian, or at least they would despoil me of the treasure after I had found it, if not before. For all these rea-

sons, I require that a trusty and loyal Spaniard
should accompany me, a man whose life shall be
in my power, and whom I can send to the gal-
lows with half a word ; a man, in short like you,
Juan Falgueira, who, after all, have gained nothing by robbing and murdering, since you are now
toiling here like a donkey, when with the millions
I am going to procure you, you can go to America,
to France, or to India, and enjoy yourself, and
live in luxury, and rise in time perhaps to be
king.   What do you think of my plan ? "

"That it is well put together, like the work of
a Moor," responded Ben-Munuza, in whose nervous hands, clasped behind his back, the iron
bar swung back and forth like a tiger's tail.

Manos-gordas smiled with satisfaction, thinking that his proposition was already accepted.

"But," added the sombre Galician, "there is
one thing you have not considered."

"And   what   is   that ? "   asked   Ben-Carime,
throwing back his head with a comical expression, and fixing his eyes on vacancy, like one who
is prepared to hear some trivial and easily answered objection.

"You have not considered that I should be an
unmitigated fool if I were to accompany you to
Spain to put you in possession of half a treasure,
relying upon your putting me in possession of the
other half.   I say this because you would only
have to say half a word the day we arrived at

Aldeire, and you thought yourself free from danger, to rid yourself of my company and avoid giving me my half of the treasure, after it was found. In truth, you are not the clever man you imagine yourself to be, but only a simpleton deserving of pity, who have deliberately walked into a trap from which there is no escape, in telling me where this great treasure is to be found, and telling me at the same time that you know my history, and that if I were to accompany you to Spain you would there be absolute master of my life. And what need, then, have I of you? What need have I of your help to go and take possession of the entire treasure myself? What need have I of you in the world at all? Who are you, now that you have read me that document, now that I can take it from you?"

"What are you saying?" cried Manos-gordas, who all at once felt a chill, like that of death, strike to the marrow of his bones.

"I am saying—nothing. Take that!" replied Juan Falgueira, dealing Ben-Carime a tremendous blow on the head with the iron bar. The Moor rolled over on the ground, the blood gushing from his eyes, nose, and mouth, without uttering a single sound.

The unfortunate man was dead.

XII.

THREE or four weeks after the death of Manos-gordas, somewhere about the 20th of February, 1821, it was snowing, if it ever were to snow, in the town of Aldeire, and throughout the beautiful Andalusian sierra to which the snow gives existence, as it were, and a name.

It was Carnival Sunday, and the church bell was for the fourth time summoning to mass with its thin, clear tones, like those of a child, the shivering Christians of this parish (too near to heaven for their comfort), who found it difficult, on so raw and inclement a day, to bring themselves to leave their beds or to move away from the fire, saying, perhaps, in excuse for their not doing so, that on the three days before Ash-Wednesday worship should be rendered not to God, but to the devil.

Some such excuse as this, at least, was given by Uncle Juan Gomez in answer to the arguments with which his pious wife, our friend, Dame Tor-cuata, tried to persuade him to give up drinking brandy and eating biscuits, and accompany her, instead, to mass, like a good Christian, regard-less of the criticisms of the schoolmaster or the other electors of the liberal party.   And the dispute was beginning to grow warm, when suddenly Genaro, his honor's head shepherd, entered the kitchen, and taking off his hat, and scratching his head with the same movement, said:

"God give us good-day, Señor Juan and Señora Torcuata! You must have guessed already that something has happened up above to bring me down here on a day like this, it not being my Sunday for going to hear mass. I hope you are both well!"

"There! there! I'll wait no longer!" cried the Alcalde's wife, impatiently, folding her mantilla over her breast. "It was decreed that you were not to hear mass to-day. You have drink enough there, and conversation enough for the whole day, discussing the question as to whether the goats are with kid or whether the young rams are beginning to get their horns. You will go to perdition, Juan, you will go to perdition, if you don't soon make your peace with the church and give up the accursed alcalde-ship!"

When Dame Torcuata had departed, the Alcalde handed a biscuit and a glass of brandy to the head shepherd, saying:

"Women's nonsense, Uncle Genaro! Draw your chair up to the fire and tell me what you have to say. What is going on up above there?"

"Oh, a mere nothing! Yesterday, Francisco, the goat-keeper, saw a man dressed like a native of Malaga, with long trousers and a linen jacket, and wrapped in a blanket, go into the cattle-yard

you are making, from the open side, and walk
around the Moor's Tower, examining it and measuring it, as if he were a master-builder. Francisco
asked him what he was doing, to which the stranger answered by asking in his turn who was the
owner of the tower, and Francisco saying that he
was no less a person than the Alcalde of the
town, the stranger replied that he would speak
with his honor and explain his plans to him.
Night soon fell, and as the man pretended to be
going away, the goat-herd went to his hut, which,
as you know, is but a short distance from the
tower. Some two hours later the same Francisco
noticed that strange noises proceeded from the
tower, in which he also observed a light burning,
all which terrified him so greatly, that he did not
even venture to go to my hut to tell me of what
he had seen and heard. This he did as soon as
it was daylight, saying in addition that the noises
he had heard in the tower were kept up all night.
As I am an old man and have served my king
and am not easily frightened, I went at once to
the Moor's Tower, accompanied by Francisco,
who trembled at every step he took, and we discovered the stranger, wrapped up in his blanket,
asleep in a little room on the ground floor where
the plaster still remains on the ceiling. I
wakened the mysterious stranger and reproved
him for spending the night in a strange house
without its owner's permission, to which he

answered that the building was not a house, but a heap of ruins, where a poor wayfarer might very well take shelter on a snowy night, and that he was ready to present himself before you and tell you who he was and what his business and his plans were. I have brought him with me, therefore, and he is now out in the yard with the goat-herd, waiting for your permission to enter."

" Let him come in," answered Uncle Hormiga, rising to his feet, greatly disturbed, for the thought had presented itself to his mind at the head shepherd's first words, that all this was closely connected with the celebrated treasure, the hope of discovering which, by his own un-aided exertions, he had abandoned, a week before, after he had removed, without result, several of the heaviest of the foundation stones.

XIII.

Here, then, we have, face to face and alone, Uncle Juan Gomez and the stranger.

"What is your name ? " the former asked the latter, with all the imperiousness warranted by his exalted office, and without inviting him to be seated.

" My name is Jaime Olot," responded the mysterious stranger.

" You do not speak like a native of this country. Are you English ? "

" I am a Catalan."

" Ah, a Catalan! That may be. And what brings you to these parts? And, above all, what the devil were you doing yesterday measuring my tower?"

" I will tell you. I am a miner by profession, and I have come to this country, which is famous for its copper and silver mines, in search of work. Yesterday afternoon, passing by the Moor's Tower, I saw that a wall was being built with the stones that had been taken from it, and that it would be necessary to tear down a great deal more of the building in order to finish the wall. There is no one who can equal me in pulling down buildings, whether by the use of tools or with hands only, for I have the strength of an ox, and the idea occurred to me that I might be able to make a contract with the owner of the tower to pull it down and dig up the foundation stones."

Uncle Hormiga, with a wink of his little gray eyes, responded, dwelling upon every word:

" Well, that arrangement does not suit me."

" I would do the work for very little—almost nothing."

" Now it would suit me less than before."

The so-called Jaime Olot was puzzled not a little by the mysterious answers of Uncle Juan Gomez, and he tried to get some clue to their meaning from the expression of his face; but as he was unsuccessful in his efforts to read the fox-

11

like countenance of his honor, he added, with
feigned naturalness :

" It would not displease me, either, to repair
a part of the old building and to live there,
cultivating the ground that you had intended for
a cattle-yard. I will buy from you, then, the
Moor's Tower with the ground around it."

" I do not wish to sell it," responded Uncle
Hormiga.

" But I will pay you double what it is worth ! "
said the self-styled Catalan emphatically.

" It would suit me now less than ever to sell
it," replied the Andalusian, with so crafty and
insulting a look that his interlocutor took a step
backward, suddenly becoming conscious that he
was treading on false ground.

He reflected for a moment, therefore, and then
raising his head with a determined air, and clasping his hands behind his back, he said, with a
cynical laugh :

" So, then, you know that there is a *treasure*
on that ground ! "

Uncle Juan Gomez leaned over in his seat,
and scanning the Catalan from head to foot,
exclaimed with a comical air :

" What vexes me is that you, too, should
know it ! "

" And it would vex you much more if I should
tell you that I am the only person who knows it
with certainty."

"That is to say, that you know the precise spot in which the treasure is buried?"

"I know the precise spot, and it would not take me twenty-four hours to disinter all the wealth that lies hidden there."

"According to that you have in your possession a certain document—"

"Yes; I have a document of the time of the Moors, half a yard square, in which all the necessary directions to find the treasure are given."

"And tell me—this document—"

"I do not carry it about with me, nor is there any reason why I should do so, since I know it word for word by heart, both in Spanish and in Arabic. Oh, I am not such a fool as ever to deliver myself up, bag and baggage, to the enemy! So that before coming to this country I concealed the document—where no one but myself will ever be able to find it."

"In that case there is no more to be said. Señor Jaime Olot, let us come to an understanding, like two good friends," exclaimed the Alcalde, at the same time pouring out a glass of brandy for the stranger.

"Let us come to an understanding!" repeated the stranger, taking a seat without waiting for further permission, and drinking his brandy with gusto.

"Tell me," continued Uncle Hormiga, "and

tell me without lying, so that I may learn to put faith in you—"

"Ask what you wish; when it does not suit me to speak I shall be silent."

"Do you come from Madrid?"

"No. It is twenty-five years since I was in the capital, for the first and last time."

"Do you come from the Holy Land?"

"No; that is not in my line."

"Are you acquainted with a lawyer of Ugíjar, called Don Matías de Quesada?"

"No; I hate lawyers and all people who live by the pen."

"Well, then, how did this document fall into your possession?"

Jaime Olcot was silent.

"I like that! I see you don't want to lie!" exclaimed the Alcalde. "But there cannot be a doubt that Don Matías de Quesada cheated me as if I were a Chinese, stealing from me two ounces in gold, and then selling that document to some one in Melilla or Ceuta. And the fact is, although you are not a Moor, you look as if you had lived in those countries."

"Don't fatigue yourself, or lose your time guessing further. I will set your doubts at rest. This lawyer you speak of must have sent the manuscript to a Spaniard in Ceuta, from whom it was stolen three weeks ago by the Moor from whose possession it passed into mine."

"Ah! now I see. He must have sent it to a nephew of his who is a musician in the cathedral of that city—one Bonafacio de Tudela."

"It is very likely."

"What a wretch that Don Matías is! To cheat his gossip in this way! But see how chance has brought the document back to my hands again!"

"To mine, you would say," observed the stranger.

"To ours!" returned the Alcalde, again filling the glasses. "Why, then, we are millionaires. We will divide the treasure equally between us, since you cannot dig in that ground without my permission, nor can I find the treasure without the help of the document which has fallen into your possession. That is to say, that chance has made us brothers. From this day forth you shall live in my house—another glass—and the instant we have finished breakfast, we will begin to dig."

The conference had reached this point when Dame Torcuata returned from mass. Her husband told her all that had passed, and presented to her Don Jaime Olot. The good woman heard with as much fear as joy the news that the treasure was on the eve of discovery, crossing herself repeatedly on learning of the treachery and baseness of her gossip, Don Matías de Quesada, and she looked with terror at

the stranger, whose countenance filled her with
a presentiment of coming misfortune.

Knowing, however, that she must give this
man his breakfast, she went into the pantry to
take from it the choicest articles it contained—
that is to say, a tenderloin with pickle sauce, and
a sausage of the last killing, saying to herself,
however, as she uncovered the jars :

" Time it is that the treasure should be discovered, for whether it is to be found or not, it has
already cost us the thirty-two dollars for the famous cup of chocolate, the long-standing friendship of our gossip, Don Matías, these fine slices
of meat, that would have made so rich a dish,
dressed with peppers and tomatoes, in the month
of August, and the having so forbidding-looking
a stranger as a guest. Accursed be treasures,
and mines, and the devils, and everything that
is underground, excepting only water and the
faithful departed ! "

XIV.

While Dame Torcuata was making these reflections to herself, as she went, with a pan in
either hand, toward the fire, cries and hisses of
women and children resounded in the street,
mingled with other voices in a lower key, saying:
" Señor Alcalde ! Open the door ! The city

authorities are entering the town with a troop of soldiers ! "

Jaime Olot became yellower than wax when he heard these words, and clasping his hands together, he said :

" Hide me, Señor Alcalde ! Otherwise we shall not find the treasure ! The authorities have come in search of me ! "

" In search of you ? And why so ? Are you a criminal ? "

" I knew it ! " cried Aunt Torcuata. " From that gloomy face no good could come. All this is the doing of Lucifer ! "

" Quick ! quick ! " resumed the stranger. " Take me out by the back door ! "

" Very good, but first give me directions where to find the treasure," said Uncle Hormiga.

" Señor Alcalde ! " the cry was repeated outside the door, " open ! The town is surrounded ! It seems it is that man who has been shut up with you for the last hour they are in search of ! "

" Open to the authorities ! " an imperious voice now cried, accompanied by a loud knocking at the door.

" There is no help for it ! " said the Alcalde, going to open the door, while the stranger tried to escape into the yard by the other door.

But the head shepherd and the goat-herd, who were on the alert, cut off his egress, and

they and the soldiers, who had now also entered
the room, seized and bound him securely, although the renegade displayed in the struggle
the strength and agility of a tiger.

The constable of the court, who had under his
command a clerk and twenty foot-soldiers, meantime told the Alcalde the causes of and reasons
for this noisy arrest.

"This man," he said, "with whom you have
been shut up I don't know why—talking of I
don't know what—is the famous Galician, Juan
Falgueira, who, fifteen years ago, robbed and
murdered a party of gentlemen, whose muleteer
he was, in a certain hamlet of Granada, and who
escaped from the chapel on the eve of the day
appointed for his execution, dressed in the habit
of the friar who was administering to him the
consolations of religion, and whom he left there
half-strangled. The king himself—whom Heaven
preserve—received, a fortnight ago, a letter from
Ceuta, signed by a Moor named Manos-gordas,
saying that Juan Falgueira, after long residence
in Orán and other points in Africa, was about to
embark for Spain, and that it would be an easy
matter to seize him in Aldeire in El Cenét, where
it was his intention to purchase a Moorish tower
and to devote himself to mining. At the same
time a communication was received by the government from the Spanish Consul in Tetuan,
stating that a Moorish woman called Zama had

presented herself before him to make complaint
against the Spanish renegade, Ben-Manuza, formerly called Juan Falgueira, who had just sailed
for Spain, after having assassinated the Moor,
Manos-gordas, the complainant's husband, and
robbed him of a certain precious document. For
all which reasons, and chiefly on account of the
attempt against the life of the friar in the chapel,
His Majesty the King strongly urged upon the
authorities of Granada the arrest of the criminal
and his immediate execution in that city."

Let the reader picture to himself the terror and
astonishment with which this narration was listened to by all present, as well as the despair of
Uncle Hormiga, who could not now doubt that
the document was in the possession of this man
condemned to death.

The avaricious Alcalde, then, at the risk of
compromising himself still further, called aside
Juan Falgueira and held a whispered conversation
with him, having previously informed the assem-
blage that he was going to try to prevail upon the
renegade to confess his crime before God and
men.   What passed between the two *partners*,
however, was really what follows :

"Gossip ! " said Uncle Hormiga, " not Heaven
itself could now save you ! But you must feel
that it would be a pity that that document should
be lost. Tell me where you have hidden it."

"Gossip ! " responded the Galician, " with

that document, or, in other words, with the treasure it represents, I intend to purchase my pardon. Procure for me the royal favor, and I will deliver the document to you; but for the present I shall offer it to the judges to bribe them to declare my sentence null and void by prescription."

" Gossip ! " replied Uncle Hormiga, " you are a wise man, and I shall be glad if you succeed in your purpose. But if you fail, for God's sake do not carry to the tomb a secret which will profit no one ! "

" Be certain, I shall take it with me ! " answered Juan Falgueira. " I must have my revenge upon the world in some way."

" Let us proceed ! " here cried the constable, putting an end to this strange conference.

And the condemned man, being chained and handcuffed, the officers of justice and the soldiers proceeded with him in the direction of the city of Guadix, whence they were to conduct him to Granada.

" The devil! the devil ! " the wife of Uncle Hormiga Juan Gomez kept repeating to herself for an hour afterward, as she returned the tenderloin and the sausage to their respective jars. " My curse upon all treasures—past, present, and to come ! "

XV.

NEEDLESS to say that Uncle Hormiga found no
means of procuring Juan Falgueira's pardon, nor
did the judges condescend to listen seriously to
the offers which the latter made them of deliver-
ing to them a treasure on condition that they
should relinquish the prosecution against him;
nor did the terrible Galician consent to disclose
the hiding-place of the document nor the where-
abouts of the treasure to the bold Alcalde of
Aldeire—who, with this hope, had the face to
visit him in the chapel in the prison of Granada.

Juan Falgueira, then, was hanged on the Friday preceding Good Friday, in the Paseo del
Triumfo, and Uncle Hormiga, on his return to
Aldeire, on Palm Sunday, fell ill with typhoid
fever, the disease running its course so quickly
that on Wednesday of Holy Week he confessed
himself and made his will and expired on the
morning of Easter Saturday.

But before his death he wrote a letter to Don
Matías de Quesada, reproaching him with his
treachery and dishonesty (which had caused the
deaths of three persons), and forgiving him like a
Christian, on condition that he should return to
Dame Torcuata the thirty-two dollars for the cup
of chocolate.

This dreadful letter reached Ugíjar simultane-
ously with the news of the death of Uncle Juan

Gomez, both which events, coming together, affected the old lawyer to such a degree that he never recovered his spirits again, and he died shortly afterward, having written in his last hour a terrible letter, full of reproaches and maledictions, to his nephew, the Chapel-master of Ceuta, accusing him of having deceived and robbed him, and of being the cause of his death.

To the reading of this just and tremendous accusation was due, it is said, the stroke of apoplexy that sent Don Bonifacio to the tomb.

So that the suspicion, merely, of the existence of a hidden treasure was the cause of five deaths, and of many other misfortunes, matters remaining in the end as hidden and mysterious as they were in the beginning, since Dame Torcuata, who was the only person in the world who knew the history of the fatal document, took good care never to mention it thereafter in the whole course of her life, thinking, as she did, that it had all been the work of the devil, and the necessary consequence of her husband's dealings with the enemies of the Church and the Throne.

BREAD CAST UPON THE WATERS

BY

FERNAN CABALLERO

Translated by Mary J. Serrano.

BREAD CAST UPON THE WATERS

BY FERNAN CABALLERO

CHAPTER I.

ALTHOUGH the villages of the sierras of Andalusia, owing to their elevation, enjoy in summer a milder temperature than those of the plains, during the middle hours of the day the sun, reflected from the rocks that abound in this mountainous region, produces a dry and ardent heat, which is more transitory, indeed, but also more irritating than that of the plains. The chief sufferers from its ardors are the wandering reapers, who, after finishing the labors of the harvest in their own province, go in search of work to the provinces where the harvest has not yet been gathered in. The greater number of the reapers of the province of Granada go to the sierra of Ronda, where they are welcomed, and where their toilsome labors are well rewarded, so that they are able to lay by some money, unless indeed sickness, that scourge of the poor, prostrates them and consumes their earnings or terminates their existence.

In a more pious age a small hospital for poor strangers was established in Bornos, which is one of the villages that, like a fringe, border the slope of the sierra; an hospital which remained closed in winter, but which in summer received many of the poor reapers who were prostrated by the intense heat, and who had no home or family in the village.

On a hot summer day, early in the thirties, a woman with a kind and gentle countenance was seated at the door of her cottage, in the village above mentioned, engaged in chopping the tomatoes and peppers and crumbling the bread for the wholesome, nutritious, and savory gazpacho which was to serve for the family supper; her two children, a boy of seven and a girl of five, were playing not far from her in the street.

As Bornos is almost entirely surrounded by orchards and orange groves, planted on the slopes of the tableland on which the village is seated, and which at this hour are irrigated by the clear and abundant waters of its springs, every breeze brought with it the perfume of the leaves and the melodious strains of the birds singing their evening hymn to the sun, filling the air with coolness, as if kind Mother Nature made of her trees a fan to cool the brow of her favorite child, man. The front of the house was already steeped in shadow, while the sun still gilded the irregular crests of the mountains on the opposite side of

the valley that, like patient camels, supported
the load of vines, olive groves, and cornfields
confided to them by man.

The mother, occupied with her task, had
not observed that a poorly clad little boy had
joined her children and that they were talking
together.

"Who are you?" said the Bornos boy to the
stranger; "I have never seen you before.   What
is your name?"

"Michael; and yours?"

"Gaspar."

"And my name is Catherine," said the little
girl, who desired also to make the strange boy's
acquaintance.

"I know the story of St. Catherine," said the
latter.

"Oh, do you?   Tell it to us."

The boy recited the following verses :

"To-morrow will be St. Catherine's day,
  When to heaven she will ascend and St. Peter will say,
  'What woman is that who asks to be let in?'
  'I am Catherine,' she will answer, 'and I want to come
  in.'
  'Enter, little dove, in your dove-cote, then.' "

"What a lovely story!" exclaimed the girl.
"Don't you know another?"

"Look, Catherine," cried her brother, who was
eating roasted beans; "there is a little dead
snail in this bean, a roasted snail."

12

"Will you give me some beans?" begged the strange child.

"Yes, here are some.   Are you very, very fond of roasted beans?"

"Yes, very; but I asked you for them because I am very hungry."

"Why, have you had no dinner?"

"No."

"Nor any breakfast, either?"

"No."

"Mother, mother," cried both the children together, running to their mother; "this poor little boy has n't had any dinner or any breakfast, and he is very hungry; give us some bread for him."

"He has had no dinner, you say?" said the good woman, giving the child a piece of bread with that compassionate tenderness which seems innate in women toward children; "have you no parents, then, my child?"

"Yes, but they have no bread to give me."

"Poor little boy!   And where are your parents?"

"Over there," answered the boy, pointing in the direction of a lane that ran between garden walls, at right angles with the street.

The good woman, followed by the children, went to the lane.

On the dry grass, with his face turned to the wall, lay a man, miserably clad and apparently lifeless; a handkerchief was tied round his head; near him lay a sickle that had fallen from his nerveless grasp; seated on the ground beside him was a woman, who, with her thin cheek resting on her emaciated hand, was gazing fixedly at him through the tears that rolled down her sad face, as on a rainy day the water trickles down the walls of a deserted ruin. The last rays of the setting sun, lingering in the lane, illumined the melancholy group with a light tender and sorrowful as a farewell glance.

Approaching the stranger, the good woman, whose name was Maria, said to her:

" Señora, what is the matter with your husband? "

" He has a fever that is killing him," answered the stranger, bursting into sobs.

" Holy Mary! " cried the mother of the children compassionately. " And why don't you let people know about it and ask them to help you? Are we living in a heathen land, then? "

" I don't know any one in the place."

"No matter; for a neighborly act, acquaintance is n't necessary. What! Is this poor man to be left alone to die, as if he were among the Moors? Not if I can prevent it."

At this moment a man with a strong, calm, and kind face approached the group.

" Father, father," cried the children, " this

man is dying, and this little boy, who is his son, says he has no bread to give him."

"John Joseph," added the mother of the children, "this poor man is lying shelterless here; this is pitiful. If you are willing, let us carry him into the house and send for the doctor."

"Willing? Of course I am willing," answered her husband. "I have never yet refused my help to any one in need of it, God be praised! There has always been a corner in my kitchen for the poor, and especially for those who are looking for a shelter for the night, who are on a journey, or who are sick; and such food as I had, I have always shared with them! Don't you know that, wife?"

"Come, then," said the latter; "let us lift him up, John Joseph; I'll take hold of him by one arm and his wife can take him by the other."

They did as she said. One of the children took the sickle, another the hat, the third a small shabby bundle of clothes, and all went toward the house.

A sheepskin and a pair of sheets were spread over one of the thick reed mattings which serve the laborers in the farms and vineyards as beds, and the sick man, who remained sunk in a profound stupor, was placed on it, while Gasparito, who was told to fly, ran for the doctor. When the latter came, he pronounced the patient to be dangerously ill, and prescribed various medicines, which were administered to him with that zeal and intelligence in caring for the sick that is one of the many prerogatives of the sex called the fair, but which might with much more propriety be called the pious sex.

After the medicines had been administered and he had been bled freely, the patient seemed somewhat better, and sank into what seemed a natural and beneficent sleep ; and then, and not until then, did the family think of their supper, the refreshing and nutritious gaspacho, and the fruits, so abundant in the country, and of which the people, frugal, refined, and elegant, even in their material appetites, are so fond.

CHAPTER II.

It is needless to say that those first called to partake of the *mess*, as the master of the house, who had been a soldier, called it, were the strange woman and her son.

" And what part of the country are you from ? " said John Joseph to his guest, as he offered her a slice of a magnificent watermelon, which sparkled like a garnet in the light.

"From Treveles, in the Alpujarras," she answered.

" I was there when I served the king," responded John Joseph. " Those are poor villages.

Treveles is a village overhanging the ravine of Poqueira."

"That is true," replied the poor woman, whose sorrowful face brightened a little at the recollection, so dear to the heart, of the place where she was born and where her home was.

"And by the same token," continued John Joseph, "you can see from there the peaks of Mulhá Hasem and Veleta, that don't reach the sky because the Almighty would n't let them, and not because they did n't try."

"And why do they call that peak the Veleta,* John Joseph? Is it because it has one on it?"

"If it has, I never saw it."

"It has none now," said the stranger, "but it had one in former times, when Moors and Christians went fighting one another through the mountains. It was guarded by an angel who kept it pointed toward Spain, and then the Christians conquered; but if he neglected his task, the devil came and made it point toward Barbary, and then the Moors conquered."

"But, in spite of all the devil could do, we drove them out; yes, and we would have done it if there had been ten times as many of them!" said the ex-soldier.

"And were you ever on those peaks?" said the mistress of the house to her guest.

"I was never there myself," answered the

* A weather-vane.

latter ; " but my Manuel has been there a hundred times. Once he went there with an English-man who wanted to see them. Between the two peaks there is a ravine that is full of water ; and that is a cauldron that the demons made. From the middle of it come strange sounds that are caused by the hammering of the demons mending the cauldron. The whole place is a desert, full of naked rocks, and so awesome and solitary that the Englishman said it was like the Dead Sea—a sea that it seems there is in some of those far-off countries."

" Oh, mother ! and why did it die ? " asked the girl.

" How should I know ? " answered the mother.

" Father," said the girl, repeating her question : " why did that sea die ? Did the Moors kill it ? "

" What a question ! " returned the father, who did not wish to confess his ignorance of the matter, as his wife had done : " it died because everything in the world dies, even the seas."

" And is the whole mountain like that ? " asked Maria.

" No, for lower down there are trees,—chestnuts, oaks and shrubs, and some fine apple trees planted by the Moors, whose fruit is sent to Granada to be sold."

" And I was told," continued John Joseph, " that there are wild goats there that run faster than water down a hill, that leap like grasshoppers, and that are so sagacious that they always station one of their number on a height to keep watch, and when danger is approaching he strikes the rock with his foot, and then the others scamper off and disappear like a flight of partridges."

"That is all true," responded the guest; "and there are owls there, too, a kind of birds with wings and a human face."

"What is that you are saying, Señora?" cried John Joseph, "who ever saw such birds as those?"

"My Manuel has seen them, and every one who has ever climbed up those heights; and you must know that the owls and the mountain-goats have been there ever since the time when Jesus was in the world. He came to those solitudes, that were then shady meadows in which tame and handsome goats browsed, watched by their shepherds. The Lord, who was tired, entered a goat-herd's hut, and asked the goat-herds to prepare a kid for supper for Himself and St. John and St. Peter, who were with Him. The goat-herds, who were wicked Moors, said that they had none; but the Lord insisted, and then what did those heartless wretches do? They killed a cat, cooked it, and set it on the table. But the Lord, as you may suppose, who sees into all hearts and knows everything that is going on, however secret it may be thought, knew perfectly well

what the goat-herds had done, and sitting down
at the table He said:

> ' If you are a kid,
> Remain fried.
> But if you are a cat,
> Jump from the plate.'

"Instantly the animal straightened itself up
and ran off. The Lord, to punish the goat-herds,
turned them into owls and their flocks into wild
goats."

At this moment a moan was heard; they all
hurried to the sick man's bedside. His improve-
ment had been only momentary; the fever,
caused by a cerebral attack, had reached its
height, and in a few hours terminated his life,
without his having returned to consciousness for
a single instant.

It is an easy matter to describe a violent and
noisy grief which rebels against misfortune; but
it is not easy to describe a profound, silent,
humble, and resigned grief. The poor widow
who had lost everything, even the strength to
work, raised her eyes to heaven, clasped her
hands and bowed her head, while her life, which
her chilled heart was unable to maintain, slowly
ebbed away.

She was not sent away by the kind and charitable people who had sheltered her; but she
knew that she would be a heavy burden upon
them; and although she was submissive to the

will of the Lord, she prayed to Him to grant her a speedy and contrite end, as a release from all her sufferings ; and the Lord granted her prayer.

One night she saw with ineffable joy the bed on which she lay surrounded by kind, devout, and compassionate souls ; the house was lighted up ; an altar stood in front of her humble cot, on which she saw the image of our Lord, to whom she had prayed, with arms opened to those who call upon Him.   Every one brought flowers, those universal interpreters of human feeling, which enhance the splendor of the most august solemnities and lend poetry and beauty to the gayest festival ; and which, as if they were angels' gifts, are found, like these, in the hut and in the palace, in royal gardens and in the fields.

A bell sounded in the distance that with its silvery voice seemed to say : " Here cometh the Lord, who giveth a peaceful death."

And thus it was ; for when the solemn act of receiving the Last Sacrament was ended, the sick woman raised her eyes, in which a gleam of her lost happiness shone.

" I am leaving this valley of tears," she said, in a faint voice, " and through the mercy of God I am going to His presence to ask Him to watch over this poor boy, this poor orphan—"

" Orphan, did you say ? " cried John Joseph. " Don't you know, then, that he is our son ? "

The dying woman leaned her pale face against

her son's forehead, on which a tear fell, and said to him, "Child of my heart, pay to our benefactors your own debt and that of your parents; as for me, I can only pray to God that He will bless them as I bless them."

"John Joseph," said the priest, "the blessing of the dying is the most precious legacy they can leave to those who survive them."

CHAPTER III.

In 1853, Gaspar and Michael, who had grown up together like two brothers, had arrived at the age of manhood; and they were as honest and industrious as the father who had guided them. Catherine was a beautiful girl, as modest and as diligent as the mother at whose side she had grown up. Michael, who had a noble and affectionate, and consequently a grateful heart, loved the family who had adopted him with ardent affection; but especially did he love Catherine, for whom he felt all the affection of a brother, joined to all the tenderness of a lover toward her whom he desired to make the companion of his life.

Many days of tranquil happiness were enjoyed by these united and worthy people; but as happiness, like the blue of the sky, cannot be lasting, for the earth, to yield its fruits, requires the rain, and man, to estimate at their true value this

life and the next, has need of tears, a time came
in which many were shed in this house, to prove
to its inmates that God bestows this blessing,
almost preferably, on the poor and the righteous.

The draft was proclaimed and both sons were
enrolled for the drawing.

Those who know how passionate is the affection which the mothers of the people have for
their children can understand Maria's inconsolable grief.   She believed that she loved both sons
equally ; she feared for both with the same anguish ; with the same fervor she prayed to God
and to the Virgin that both might escape the
draft ; but when they returned from the drawing
and she learned that the soldier's lot had fallen
on her own son, the cry which this intelligence
drew from her mother's heart—" Child of my
soul, I knew that it must fall upon you ! "—showed
that a mother's love can be equalled by no other.

Michael saw Maria's grief with a breaking
heart, a grief which not all his own efforts nor
those of her husband could diminish or soothe.

On the following day John Joseph took his son
to the barrack, but what was the astonishment
of both when the commandant told Gaspar that
he was free and that he might return home.

" Free ! " cried Gaspar in amazement.   " And
why ? "

" Because you have a substitute," answered
the officer.

"I!" said Gaspar, with ever-increasing astonishment; "why, that can't be so!"

"Why do you say it can't be so? If the substitute is already accepted and enrolled it is so."

"But who is he?" asked Gaspar, amazed.

"That young man, there," answered the officer,
pointing to the man whom his parents, in their
beneficence, had brought up as a son.

"Michael, what have you done?" exclaimed
Gaspar, strongly moved.

"What my mother charged me on her death-
bed to do," answered Michael; "I have paid a
debt.'

"You owed me nothing," answered Gaspar;
"but I now owe you a debt; and God grant me
the opportunity to pay it, brother; if the occasion
presents itself, you may be sure I will not let it
pass; that I will not."

CHAPTER IV.

Two years after the events just recorded, a
still greater sorrow befell this worthy family, so
united and so affectionate, as the families of the
peasantry usually are. Michael drew the lot in a
second conscription, as Gaspar had done before;
and as he was thus obliged to serve on his own
account, the son of his adopted parents, whom
he could not now serve as a substitute, was once
more called to the ranks. Four years more

passed; and just when they were expecting Michael home, his time of service having expired, and while Catherine was preparing her wedding garments, a cry, uttered by the Queen of Spain, resounded through the country, electrifying the people and producing a universal outburst of patriotic enthusiasm—Long live Spain! Death to the Moor who has insulted her! This cry was re-echoed throughout the length and breadth of the Peninsula, accompanied by the clash of the warrior's sword and the chink of the rich man's gold, offered on the altar of the country's honor; it was repeated by the people, who gave their blood; by the sacred episcopate, who blessed the cause of the country and of Christianity, and whose words powerfully influenced not only timid and pious consciences, but all by their wisdom, prudence, and judgment. The Sisters of Charity offered their devoted services; the nuns made lint and sacred scapulars of the Virgin; the ladies also made lint and bandages which they moistened with their tears; and even schoolboys, fired with enthusiasm, asked to be allowed to go to the popular war against the Moors.*

* This assertion might be proved by many examples; but it will suffice to transcribe here a letter written by a nephew of mine, the son of Marquis C——

"SENOR GOVERNOR : Although I am only a boy of eight I am moved to say to you that I would like to die for the country, and that, being fond of military things, I wish

Michael, who shared in the general enthusiasm for the war, on receiving his discharge, enlisted again, refusing to accept the premium for re-enlisting, for such time as the war in Africa should last.

John Joseph, who in winter followed the occupation of a muleteer, brought home this news on his return from one of his trips, in which he had seen his sons, who were both serving in the King's regiment, in Africa.   Maria, on hearing it, burst into tears.

" They were right in saying last year, when the saddle-shaped comet appeared, that it came to foretell a war with the Moors ! " she exclaimed disconsolately.

" The comet had no resemblance to a saddle," answered her husband, with martial ardor ; " you know very well that what they said was that it was the same star that had guided the kings who went to Bethlehem to declare that Christ was the true Messiah ; very well, our people will go to the Moorish country now to tell them that Spanish Christians are tired of putting up with the atrocities and the insults of the accursed Moors."

" But a great many people will be killed in

you would permit me to go fight the Moors.—Written by P—— P——."

It is to be observed that this boy is docile, and gentle and modest in disposition, rather than daring or arrogant. —[*Note of the Author.*]

this war, John Joseph, and that is heartbreaking
to think of ; yes heartbreaking, although you with
your warlike notions say it is not."

" Oh, yes, you would like this war to be like a
war between women ; a war to the knife, but
without any one killed ; well, war with those
who use a beard, and especially if they wear the
King's uniform and have the flag of Spain, under
which they are fighting, to defend, is another
matter ; with them, the question is to conquer or
die."

" For that very reason," replied Maria disconsolately, " could n't he have come back and
stayed quietly at home, after he had fulfilled his
duty ? "

" Yes, like you, at the spinning-wheel ; but you
must know that no new sailing vessel ever yet
wanted to be a pontoon.   Don't you know that ? "

Maria and Catherine kept on crying.

" If you had even told me that you were going
to see them," said the former, " I would have
given you some scapulars to take them."

" They have them already, they have them
already, and blessed by the bishop of Malaga. I
told you before, wife, that this war is a holy
war, which will rejoice St. Ferdinand in heaven.
But you are in a crying humor, it seems," he
added impatiently, seeing that his wife and
daughter were still shedding tears.   " Why, what
would you have?   That they should remain here

like women, instead of going to throttle those accursed Moors who don't believe in Christ, who deny His Holy Mother, and who call the Spaniards 'hens' and 'Christian dogs'? But let them wait a bit, and I 'll warrant they won't want a second taste of the broth those hens will make them! They never catch a Spaniard, even in time of peace, that they don't quarter or impale him ; you see that makes every Spaniard's blood boil! I don't know how I can contain myself that I don't go too ; for I tell you that the soles of my feet are itching to go ; and the day you least expect it, I 'll take my gun and my blanket and join the camp."

" John Joseph ! In the Virgin's name ! Is n't it enough to have your sons there ? Would you leave us entirely alone ? "

" It would n't be for long."

" Hush, hush ! God only knows how long it might be ; for those people are in their own country, defending their homes ; and you know that they are ferocious, savage, fearless, and valiant."

" That they are, but as far as being fearless and valiant is concerned, we Spaniards are more so."

" And God knows what hunger and privation they are going to suffer ! "

" Don't imagine it ; but even if it should be so, give the Spanish soldier plenty of water to drink

13

and he has all he needs. Why, the joy of that regiment as they went on board was plain to be seen! And to think that I could n't have gone with them!"

"John Joseph, in the Virgin's name, don't indulge in those boyish explosions; remember, you are sixty-five years old."

"To-day I am twenty, wife, I am twenty; do you hear?"

"Your fiery spirit deceives you; and I won't hear you talk about going to the war, when you have two sons in it already."

"And if I had more sons they should be in it, too. Do you think that I should be behind the father of the first soldier killed at the taking of the Serrallo, who when he heard of his son's death called another son, took him to the alcalde of his village, and said: 'My son has been killed in the war in Africa; here is another to take his place'?"

"From what you say, I should n't wonder if you had urged Michael to go to the war?"

"Michael did n't need any urging, Michael has done well, and so I told him. 'Go without fear,' I cried to him, as I came away, 'the weather-vane in your village points for Spain; and don't lose heart, if there should be some reverse, for reverses there must be in war, unless it be by a miracle of God; but many there won't be; and the devil will have little chance to get at the weather-vane of the peak of the Alpujarras, for the one who has charge of it now is an archangel, your patron saint, Michael, and the patron saint of Spain, and he won't neglect his business, and he knows how to keep the devil at a respectful distance ! "

CHAPTER V.

Not long afterward, John Joseph went with his mule for a load of pears to Ronda. He found that from there he could go without much difficulty to the Christian camp in Africa. " Why, then," he said to himself, " I can sell my pears there as well as in Jerez or Malaga ; there I will go, then ; in that way I shall see my boys and the fighting that is going on, which will be something worth seeing." And so he went.

Catherine and Maria were far from suspecting anything of this when, six or eight days later, John Joseph returned home. After he had taken the mule to the stable and put away his things with much deliberation, he sat down and said to his wife and daughter :

" The boys send many remembrances, and hope that when you receive them you will be enjoying as good health as they are enjoying at present."

" Why, what are you saying, John Joseph ? "

" I am saying that the boys have sent you many remembrances."

" Have you had a letter from them ? "

" No, I am the letter myself."

" You !   Why, what do you mean by that ? "

" That I went to Morocco and have come back again without losing my way, with my mule Orejero, who showed little surprise when, on arriving in that strange country, we found ourselves in the midst of noise and confusion—Moors everywhere, bands playing, guns firing."

" Holy Mary !   And what did you go there for, rash man ? "

" To sell some pears that I got an excellent price for ; to see the boys, whom I found in good health and as gay as larks ; and to kill three Moors who will never again call any Spaniard 'Christian dog.'   So you see, wife, that I have not lost my journey."

" And you did that ?   God help us !   God help us ! " cried the good woman, crossing herself. " You killed three Moors, did you say ?   You would not have been able to do that unless they had been unarmed, or had been taken prisoners, or had surrendered ; and you did that ? "

" Maria, what are you saying ? " responded her husband.   " Don't you know that to kill an unarmed man would be contrary to the laws of honor and the work of an executioner ?   Don't you know that to kill a man who had surrendered would be a vile deed and would be to make one's self a butcher of men ?   Don't you know that to

kill a man who asks quarter would be the deed
of a miscreant and a coward, and would disgrace
the name of Christian and dishonor the name of
Spaniard ?   In honorable combat I killed them,
Maria, when with arms in their hands they tried
to kill me and my companions.   I know well that
the glory is not in killing but in conquering the
enemy, and I would n't want at the hour of my
death to have to remember killing any man by
treachery.   I tell you, so help me God, that I
killed them honorably, like a brave man, and may
they all die thus, for they won't surrender, not
even with the bayonet at their breasts."

"Mercy !" cried Maria, "and why not?"

"Because their holy men have made them
believe that the Spaniards are as ferocious as
themselves, and that we burn alive the wounded
and the prisoners we take. You thought that
only young chaps were good for the war, and that
I, with my sixty-five years, would be of no use in
it ; well, you were mistaken, you see, you were
mistaken, for I am of good quality, and although
the steel is worn off, the iron remains. Do you
understand ?   And I am a brave soldier, but not
an assassin, do you understand?"

"Forgive me, John Joseph, I did n't stop to
think—"

"It is plain you did n't stop to think ; and you
did n't remember, either, that your husband is
a Christian of the old stock, and a well-born

Spaniard, and that he knows how to fight the
enemies of his faith, of his country, and of his
queen ; but that he will never dishonor himself by
killing a defenceless man, nor debase himself by
putting to death a man who has surrendered, nor
make a tiger of himself by refusing his life to
a man who asks it, not even if he were Barabbas
himself."

"Were ours winning, John Joseph?"

"To be sure they were.   Winning all the time,
past, present, and future."

"But I have heard them say that a great many
more Moors are coming, with a brother of their
king, whom they call Muley Abbas."

"Let them come !   That is just what we want;
but don't imagine that those Moors that are with
the king are like the Riff Moors, who are the
most savage and the fiercest of all the Moors.
But all of them together could do nothing against
the division of Echagüe, which has covered itself
with glory in the war.   Queen Isabel may well
be proud of her soldiers.   But as I was telling
you, when I arrived at Algeciras I embarked
with my mule and my pears ; and you know that
I have no fancy for travelling by sea; for the
mule that falls on that road does n't get up again.
I landed at Ceuta and from there I went with
my mule and my pears to the camp ; and when
I saw the flag of Spain floating over the Serrallo,
my heart swelled so that my breast could hardly

contain it. I reached the camp and sold my
pears like lightning, for there is no want of money
there, nor of the will to spend it. What a hub-
bub, Maria! It seemed like the gayest kind of
a fair; nothing was to be heard but the twang
of guitars, singing, and hurrahs for the queen. I
need only tell you that the commander-in-chief
has had to forbid so much singing and guitar
playing at night, because it served as a guide to
the accursed Moors. I was just inquiring for the
King's regiment, when the bugle sounded, our
soldiers seized their guns, crying, 'Long live
Spain!' and advanced to the attack. I left my
mule there and followed them; and you may believe me that the sight was worth seeing, and
one that would have set the blood coursing in a
dead man's veins. Each of our soldiers was a
Bernardo, every officer a Pizarro, every general
a Cid. One might have thought that Santiago
himself, on his white horse, was at the head of
the army, so completely did they rout the Moors,
who are all warriors, and who were three times
as many as we. I could not tell you all I saw,
not if I had a hundred tongues. I saw General Quesada seize a gun and lead the bayonet
charge himself. 'Ah, brave son of a brave
father!' I said to myself; for I had served under
his father, and he was another of the right kind.
But why do I say another, when they are all of
the right kind! I saw the bullets flying over

the head of the commander-in-chief, as thick as
comfits in Carnival. I saw the regiment of
Granada, with its valiant commander, Colonel
Trillo, at its head, make a bayonet charge crying,
' Long live the Queen ! ' that made the Moors fly
in terror from the field ; and I heard the commander-in-chief say to the colonel, that that exploit deserved a decoration ; to which the generous colonel replied : ' Nothing for me, General,
the credit belongs to my battalion.' I heard the
commander-in-chief say to a group of soldiers
of the Granada regiment, ' How goes it, boys?
Have you received your baptism yet ? ' ' Yes,
General,' answered the soldiers, 'and the Moors
have paid dear for the christening.' In short,
Maria, if I was to tell you of all I saw there, I
should keep on talking till the Day of Judgment.
But the ones I never lost sight of, Maria, were
our two boys; and you may imagine how well
they must have fought when the commander-in-
chief, who was near by, observed them, and going
up to Michael, he said, ' You have fought well.
Now tell me, what do you wish ? ' ' To keep on
fighting, General,' answered Michael ; and on the
instant the general gave him the cross of St.
Ferdinand. I cannot tell you how I felt ; but I
thought I should go out of my wits with joy ; I
could not contain myself, and I was running to
embrace him, when I saw one of those crazy
howlers stab one of our soldiers, who fell down

beside me. ' So ? ' I said, seizing the wounded man's gun ; 'you won't have a chance to kill another brave Christian ; ' and with that I despatched him ; and as I had joined the dance, I despatched two others, and I made a bayonet charge with the boys that put wings to the feet of the Moors, for if they have a heavy hand for the fight they have a light foot for flight. Then, night coming on, I gave up the gun and went to look for my mule, who evidently had not found that dance of Moors and Christians to his liking, and who, I learned on inquiry, had gone, like a mule of peace, to the shelter of the walls of Ceuta.

"That night a storm arose that I don't believe had its equal since the world began. I thought the sea, the wind, and the rain together would bring the world to an end. But the next morning we were all as if nothing had happened, and if the devil had sent that, and others like it, at the instance of his friend, Mahoma, to terrify his enemies, they might both have been convinced that Spaniards are not to be terrified either by the roaring of the elements or the howling of their ferocious Moors.

"Well, as I was saying, next morning I got up and walked to the camp to have a chat with the boys ; for, as I have told you, the Moors had prevented me from doing so the day before. When I arrived I found the King's regiment drawn up

in line, with its band and all!   'What may this be
for?' I said to myself.   The sentry on guard was
as mute and as motionless as a statue, so that it
is n't because there are Moors in sight.   And
why is this regiment drawn up and not the others?
This was beginning to excite my curiosity.   I
drew near.   The band was playing away when
the colonel, taking his place in front of the regiment, commanded silence, and said in a loud
voice, so that all might hear him:

"'The commander-in-chief has learned with
great satisfaction that on the afternoon of the
24th of November, a soldier of the King's regiment, which I have the honor to command, seeing his companion and friend wounded and in
the hands of the Moors, and animated by the
noblest sentiments, fixed his bayonet, and throwing himself heroically upon the Moors, and striking down those who attempted to stop him, seized
his wounded friend, threw him over his shoulder,
more regardful of his friend's life than of his own,
and, snatching him from certain death, carried
him back to the ranks; and desiring to recom-
pense, in view of the whole regiment, the soldier
who, in so admirable a manner, unites in himself
the gallantry of the soldier and the piety of the
Christian, transmits to him this gold medal, which
the Cadiz Athenæum has provided and caused to
be engraved, with the object of making it an
honorable reward for an act of surpassing merit,

to be given to him before his regiment drawn up in line, so that it may serve as a stimulus to the brave and generous soldier referred to—' "

The old man's voice, up to this time so animated, here failed him, and he was unable to proceed.

"Well," said his wife, deeply moved by the story she had been listening to, "why do you stop, John Joseph? Go on."

"I can't get the words out, there's a lump in my throat; for the soldier whose name was called and who stepped from the ranks to receive the gold medal was—"

"Was who? Why do you stop?"

"He was—my son. He was Gaspar!"

"Child of my heart! And the Virgin has kept him safe for me!" cried Maria.

"My darling brother! And he saved Michael's life!" murmured Catherine.

"And he killed three Moors! Ah, good son, honor of my gray hairs!" added John Joseph, with enthusiastic tenderness.

There was a moment's silence during which tears choked the utterance of these simple people, and they could only clasp their hands and raise their eyes to heaven.

When he had somewhat recovered from his emotion, John Joseph continued his recital in these words:

"When the ceremony was over I went in

search of my boys. I cannot describe, Maria,
what I felt when I saw them, the one with his gold
medal and the other with his cross of St. Ferdinand. But what I can say is that the queen
herself can't feel prouder, with her crown and
sceptre, than I felt with my Gaspar and my
Michael! If Gaspar was happy, Michael was
happier still; his eyes danced with joy; the
other seemed dazed. 'Good, my son, good,' I
said to him, 'that's the way Spaniards behave
when they are fighting for their country, their
queen, and their faith, remembering that the
soldier who is brave and not humane is brave
only as the brutes are. You have deserved the
medal, son, and your father's blessing with it.'"

"'Why, what did I do?' said Gaspar, who
like all really brave men is neither proud nor
boastful, and holds himself for less, not more
than he is really worth.

"'You saved your brother's life,' I replied.

"'And by so heroic an act that it will be
written in letters of gold,' added Michael.

"'Why, nonsense,' answered Gaspar, putting
his arm around his brother's neck ; ' I have done
nothing but pay a debt I owed.'

"'And Spain has paid the debt she owed to
the Moors, and with interest,' I said ; and I fancy
they won't be likely to try their tricks again. So
you see, wife, all the advantages the war has
brought us. Hurrah for the war !"

"John Joseph," returned his wife, "we must n't forget, because it has been favorable to us—and that, perhaps, owing to that poor mother's dying blessing—the many evils to which war gives rise : the unhappy people who suffer, those who are left disabled, those who die, and all the families who are at this moment weeping and in mourning; for war is a calamity, and therefore we ought to pray to God with all our hearts and souls for peace, for the song of the angels is : 'Glory to God in the highest; and peace on earth, to men of goodwill!'"

CHAPTER VI

Two months later, that is to say, toward the middle of January, John Joseph, his wife, and his daughter were seated one evening around the brazier. The sky had been covered for several days with heavy clouds that sent down their rain with a steadiness not usual in storms. The wind that came from the Levant roared as if it brought with it, to terrify Spain, the menacing howls of the savage children of Africa and the growling of its lions.

"Who knows what they may be going through now!" said Catherine, in a voice choked with emotion.

"Ah, merciful God," answered her mother, "with swamps for a floor, tents that let the water through for shelter, and the cholera killing them by hundreds, and the Moors lying in ambush for them or treacherously following them, and those eternal nights that swallow up the days! There is no strength nor courage that could bear up against so many ills."

"And that is not the worst," said John Joseph, with the thoughtless frankness of the peasant, bringing his foot heavily down on the floor and raising his eyes to heaven.

"What! There are worse things yet?" said Maria, anxious and surprised. "Why, what else is there, John Joseph? What else? Speak out."

"Hunger!" answered her husband in a funereal voice.

"Holy Mary!" cried the poor mother in terror. "What is that you say, man? And the provisions, then?"

"Provisions they cannot get there; they must be sent by sea from Spain; and although they took plenty with them, when they get used up more must be sent, and with these storms, to which there is neither stop nor stay, not even the birds could cross the Strait. Those are the chances of war, Maria; and if it has pleased God to send His storms precisely in these days it must be to put our courage and our constancy to the proof, Maria, so that we may go to Him and ask His help, and so that the victory, being more dearly bought, may be the more brilliant and the more prized."

"Or the sufferings and the death of our soldiers the more deeply felt and bitterly lamented," returned his wife. "Merciful God! Tempestuous weather, an epidemic, fierce and treacherous enemies around them, and hunger! Who would not lose heart with all this?"

"The Spanish soldier, Maria."

"And will the generals and the great people come back?"

"Neither the one nor the other, Maria. And if any of them should be obliged to come back because they are sick or wounded, it will be in grief and rage, and only because they can't help themselves; I know them, Maria, I know them."

"What, are they all going to perish, then?"

"Don't imagine it, for God and the Holy Virgin will bring them safely through; hold that for an article of faith."

"Let us ask them to do it, then," groaned the unhappy mother. "Mother of the forsaken! where are my sons? What has become of them? Are they alive? If they are, what will they not be suffering, and what will they not suffer in the future, if thou dost not protect them? How their hearts will be filled with anguish and their minds with despair! Holy Mother! if I only had news of them, even. Let us pray to the Virgin to intercede for them."

The family began to recite the rosary with that fervor which changes anguish to hope, and sorrow to resignation ; and scarcely had they ended when a little boy called out from the door :

"Uncle John Joseph, my father says there is a letter in the post-office for you, and that it is from the Christian's camp over yonder."

John Joseph, with the activity of twenty years, hurried out of the house, while Maria and her daughter, falling on their knees before an image of the Virgin, raised their clasped hands in prayer.

John Joseph soon returned, bringing with him one of his cronies who knew how to read and who proceeded to read aloud the letter which the former had carried in his trembling hand.

"MY DEAR PARENTS : I hope that when you receive this you will be enjoying as good health as I desire for myself. Michael and I are well, and at your service. The cholera is raging again, but we laugh at it. Every day of action is a day of pleasure and enjoyment for us ; for it is happiness enough for us to win glory for our country and to see the enthusiasm of everybody ; for this increases every day, as well among us of the ranks as among the officers and generals, and which shows most it would be hard to say. The mess has been a little scanty in these last days, because the sea was fiercer than the Moors themselves, and the boats were unable to reach us with the supplies ; but what matter ? The worst of it was that we had no tobacco. And so it happened that the commander-in-chief, who came among us encouraging us, like a greatly respected but very careful father, came up to me and said : ' Well, my boy, are you very hungry ? ' And I answered him : ' The hunger is nothing, General ; if I only had—if I only had a cigarette.'—And what do you think he did ?   He went to his tent and brought from it an enormous box of cigars that the Queen had presented to him for the campaign ; and saying that Her Majesty would be glad that they should serve to lighten the labors of her faithful soldiers, he distributed them among us.   We have received provisions, thanks to the navy, that on this occasion did not seem the sister but the mother of the army ; and as for that brave General Bustillo, a hundred lives, if we had them, would n't be enough to pay him for all he has done for us.   Hurrah for the navy, father, notwithstanding that your worship does n't like the sea.

"You must know, father, that a prince of the royal house of France has arrived here. Although tall and of handsome presence, he is but a boy—only seventeen. If your worship had seen him, you would have said that he was only a stripling, and not fit for such hard service, but you would have changed your mind if you had

14

seen how he attacked the Moors. On my faith I had always believed that, from Santiago down, only the Spaniards attacked the Moors in that way. We believe here that what he wanted to do was to perform another exploit like the one related by Michael's mother of Hernando del Pulgar in her native Granada, and to fasten the Ave-Maria on the tent of Don Manuel Habas, and that he would have done it, too, if he had n't been held back. And mind you, father, it is a very noble thing, and one worthy of admiration, to come, without anything obliging him to it, to this war, which is no child's play, just for the sake of proving himself brave. True it is that to have that name is worth more than all the gold in the world, and lifts one a foot above the ground.

"We have made more than half a dozen charges with the bayonet, father, like the one in which your worship took part. These charges are not, as one might say, greatly to the taste of the Moors, who, when they hear the call to the charge, to which we have given the name of General Prim's Polka, tremble and turn pale and fall back.*

* It may properly be related here that this same division, with its leader, General Prim, reconnoitring at a few leagues distance from Tetuan, came upon a poor old Moorish woman, sick and abandoned by her people; and that putting her on a stretcher, they carried her on their shoulders to Tetuan with all the gentleness of sisters of charity. —[*Note of the Author.*]

"Michael gives me many remembrances for you, and bids me tell Catherine that he does not forget her, and he bids me tell you, father, that you were right when you said that his saint would not neglect the weather-vane that has always pointed for Spain, for we have never once been defeated, and mind you that the Moors are valiant men, and that they fight with desperate courage. With this I say good-bye, asking your blessing for your son,

"GASPAR.

"Mother : I never enter action without commending myself to the Virgin, as you told me to do."

It will be easy to understand the delight of the parents on reading this cheering and animated letter, which was read many times over, for as soon as it was known in the village that a letter had arrived from Africa, the house was besieged with people eager to hear the news of the most national and popular war which Spain has had since the Independence.

CHAPTER VII.

SEVERAL days passed, and the loving mother's heart was once more a prey to anxiety.

"John Joseph," she said to her husband, "we have heard nothing, and that means that they can't take Tetuan."

"Hold your tongue, you foolish woman," answered her husband; "wherever the sun enters the Spaniards can enter. And don't you know that Zamora was n't taken in an hour, and that the artillery can't cross over swamps, and that a causeway has to be built? Women, who know nothing about war, think that to take a fortress in an enemy's country is as easy as to toss a pan-cake."

But on the 5th of February a muleteer, who came from Xerez, brought the news to Bornos, which had been transmitted to Xerez by telegraph, that a hard-fought battle had taken place the preceding day before Tetuan, in which, as in all the previous ones, the Spaniards had come off victorious, having made themselves masters of five encampments of the enemy, although at the cost of many lives.

His patriotic ardor, added to a feeling of deep anxiety, made it impossible for John Joseph to remain in the village, and he set out for Xerez. There he learned that the wounded of that memorable day were to be taken to Seville, and as a train of materials for the railroad was just leaving for that city, he begged to be taken on board.

The 7th of February dawned—a day memorable for ever in the annals of Spain. Day had scarcely broken when the sonorous and soul-stirring bells of the Cathedral of Seville, diffusing, authorizing, and solemnizing joy, announced to

the sleeping people the great and auspicious event
of the taking of Tetuan. It would be impossible
to give an idea of the impression caused by those
sounds, for who can describe the apogee of the
most unanimous, ardent, and national enthusiasm ? But let a few facts speak for themselves.

The priests who repaired to the churches to
say mass recited it solemnly in chorus, and afterward chanted the Te Deum, that august hymn
of thanks to the Lord.

The venerable Generals Guajardo and Her-
nandez, military authorities of the district, and
both veterans, in whose laurels there is not a leaf
that time can wither, when they met fell into each
other's arms, unable to utter a word ; the sight
of this noble spectacle drawing tears from the
eyes of the officers who were present.   When the
alcalde presented himself before the archbishop
to ask his consent to take in procession the image of the Immaculate Virgin, the patroness of
Spain, and the standard and sword of St. Ferdinand, the venerable Prince of the Church burst
into tears, causing the alcalde to shed tears also ;
seeing which, a man of the people rushed to the
latter, saying : " Senor Alcalde, let me embrace
your worship ! " The people called for their
venerable pastor, and the latter, showing himself
on the balcony, blessed his flock, who cheered
him enthusiastically.   The various sodalities of
women entered their magnificent chapel in pro-

cession, giving thanks aloud to the Virgin. Musicians paraded the streets, followed by a multitude intoxicated with joy, who cheered the Queen, Spain, the army, and the generals who had led it to victory, and who stopped before the houses where the commanders and officers wounded in this glorious war were lodged, to cheer them also.

In the public square, a vender of oranges abandoned his stall and his merchandise, leaving behind him a notice which said : " The owner of this stall has turned crazy with joy, and here he leaves this trash." Others broke the jars of a water-seller (the value of which they gave him promptly), saying, " What is this ? Water ? To-day nothing but wine is to be drunk in Seville." Further on, another group shouted, " No one sleeps to-night ; whoever sleeps to-night is an Englishman ! " Flags on the towers, hangings on the houses, the pleasing noise of joy everywhere.

"A telegraphic despatch," shouted the blind men, beside themselves with joy, " announcing the entrance of our valiant troops into the great city of Tetuan, and the utter annihilation of the Moors. Long live Spain ! Long live the Queen ! Long live the army ! Long live the Moors ! " " What is that you are saying, man ? Long live the Moors ? " " Yes, so that we may kill them again ! "

Such is the enthusiasm of the Spanish people
when it is unanimous, legitimate, and genuine;
they go to their churches, take out in procession
the Immaculate Virgin, cheer their queen, their
prelates, their authorities, their country, applaud
their army, which gives them power and great-
ness, its commander and the generals who lead
it, and those who bring back from the war
glorious wounds; and not even for its most
ferocious enemies does it find the odious
" Death ! "

And that you, brave soldiers who remain in
Africa, who have bestowed so great a joy upon
your country, should be unable to witness the
gratitude with which it repays you !

Perhaps the universal and frantic enthusiasm
inspired by the taking of a Moorish city, however heroic the exploit which had put it in the
power of the Spaniards, may seem dispropor-
tioned to the occasion; but this is not the case,
for in the first place, the people, with their admirable instinct, know that the result is, in everything, what gives it its value; they feel, besides,
that it is not only a Moorish city and the advantages its capture may bring, which its army has
gained for Spain, but also that from the Moorish
fire the Spanish phœnix has arisen, directing its
flight to a glorious future; and in the second
place, because in these public demonstrations,
in this ardent expansion, the country gives ex-

pression to three months of admiration, of interest, and of sympathy. This was owed to the army for its constancy, for its unequalled valor, for its boundless humanity. This debt the country owed, and it paid it in love, in admiration, and enthusiasm.

On the 8th, the same rejoicings were continued; processions, salvos, and so much firing of guns everywhere, that it was said as much powder was expended in it as in the taking of Tetuan. On the 9th, one of the principal streets of the city was named the street of Tetuan; the ceremony taking place at eight o'clock in the evening, when the municipal council went in procession to the street, carrying the Queen's likeness.

But meantime Maria had had no news of John Joseph. Exaggerated reports of the losses by which the victory had been gained were spread. Maria was unable to control her anxiety, and she set out, as many other mothers of the peasantry did, for the capital, where the wounded, who might perhaps be able to give her some news of her sons, were to be brought.

Mother and daughter reached Seville on the evening of the 9th, and after resting for a few moments at an inn, went out to inquire where the wounded, who had been recently brought to the city, had been taken.

A vast crowd of people and enthusiastic cheering announced to them the approach of the procession. They stood on a bench in a porch to watch it as it passed. Five mounted pioneers and a numerous band headed the procession; the municipal guard followed on foot; then came four men carrying flags, followed by a number of men bearing torches; and then the soldiers who had been wounded in Africa, wearing laurel wreaths and carrying ensigns with the names, in silver letters, of the principal victories gained by the army. After these came the municipal council headed by the civil governor and two councillors carrying the likeness of the Queen, and the procession was closed by a detachment of infantry with another band of music at its head.

"Here come the wounded soldiers!" cried the crowd, and the cheering became more enthusiastic, and tears ran down the cheeks of the women as they stopped to look admiringly at the wounded heroes, and then joined the procession. "Look at that one! Look at that poor fellow; he isn't able to walk alone; they are supporting him," some one said close beside Maria, pointing to a young man, who with his arm in a sling, his pale forehead crowned with laurel, and carrying in his hand an ensign bearing on it the word "Tetuan," walked with a modest expression on his thin but pleasing face, leaning on the arm of a robust old man whose proud and enraptured expression seemed to say to every one, "This brave man is

my son!" Maria, whose heart had for many
days past been agitated alternately by fear, hope,
enthusiasm, and anguish, uttered a cry drawn
from her by all these mingled feelings, as she
recognized in the emaciated and glory-covered
wounded soldier her son, and fell into Catherine's
arms.

CHAPTER VIII.

A few months later a happy wedding, the
wedding of Catherine and Michael, was celebrated
in Bornos. Gaspar, whose health was entirely
re-established, but who had lost his right arm,
was present. But if he had lost an arm he had
in return received a gold medal, a cross with a
pension attached to it, and an annuity; the last,
as having been disabled in the war in Africa;
the cross for bravery; and the medal for humane and gallant conduct.

"Every day is a day of thanksgiving! There
is not a happier father in the world than I!"
exclaimed John Joseph gayly. "My only grief is
to see you crippled, my boy. But that can't be
helped. You have paid your debt to the country
like an honest man, Gaspar."

"And the country, father," answered Gaspar,
pointing proudly to his cross and medal, "has
acquitted herself fully of hers to me."

"You are right, my son: and so, sirs, a toast.

Long live the Queen, and long live all the generous and patriotic Spaniards who, like Her Majesty and the Royal Family, have aided in taking care of the wounded and disabled soldiers of the African war ! "

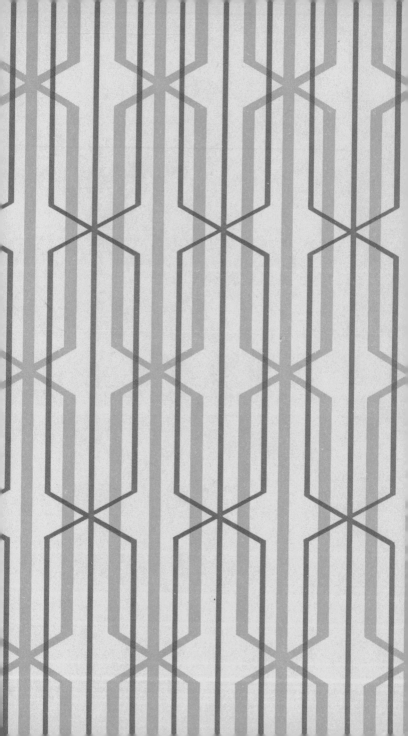